LOVE IN THE TIME OF CHAOS

'A poet's work is to name the unnameable, to point at frauds, to take sides, start arguments, shape the world, and stop it going to sleep.'
— Salman Rushdie, *The Satanic Verses*

Rosemary Jenkinson

LOVE IN THE TIME OF CHAOS

ARLEN
HOUSE

Love in the Time of Chaos

is published in 2023 by

ARLEN HOUSE
42 Grange Abbey Road
Baldoyle
Dublin D13 A0F3
Ireland
Email: arlenhouse@gmail.com
www.arlenhouse.ie

ISBN 978–1–85132–299–2, paperback

International distribution:
SYRACUSE UNIVERSITY PRESS
621 Skytop Road, Suite 110
Syracuse
New York 13244–5290
USA
Email: supress@syr.edu
www.syracuseuniversitypress.syr.edu

Typesetting by Arlen House

Cover image by Patrick Fitzsimons

CONTENTS

ACKNOWLEDGEMENTS

Thanks to Damian Smyth of the Arts Council of Northern Ireland for instilling in me that writing is the only way. Thanks also to Alan Hayes for his huge support of me personally and for publishing three of my books in the past year. Kudos to Cathy McCullough for our trip to the Himalayan Echoes Festival. Thanks to Yasya Golovko, Ryan and Rab.

Many thanks to Michael Shannon and BBC Radio 4 Short Works for broadcasting 'Oestrogen City' in April 2022.

Special thanks to Patrick Fitzsimons for his painting on the front cover.

Thanks to copyright holders for text from 'Echo Beach' by Martha and the Muffins, written by Mark Gane.

LOVE IN THE TIME OF CHAOS

'All those who actually live the mysteries of life
haven't the time to write, and all those who have
the time don't live them! D'you see?'

– Nikos Kazantzakis, *Zorba the Greek*

THE CROSSHAIR

It was the death of Kurtis McCrea's mother that made him think of going public. That was the catalyst, the freedom of expression that came with a mother's demise. 'Don't make a show of us' had always been his mother's motto whenever he talked too loudly in the street. A show! There was vanity in the word, as if she thought herself worthy of being the lead in a TV reality show. Not that it was only her. All the families in his street were bound with the light gag of a city that kept too many secrets. Everyone knew what was going on and no one could talk about it except in the briefest of doorstep whispers.

But now she was dead and it was odd how a woman who wanted to be low-key all her life was dressed up in her coffin as a parade of friends, family, acquaintances and people who had hardly heard tell of her filed into the living room to see her. Now, this was a woman who had never wanted a party thrown for her birthday yet had insisted on a wake, just as her own parents had been waked. An hour before the funeral cortege set off there were queues waiting outside her front door to have a nosey, since open caskets were a rare treat these days. What are you all queuing for, a freakshow, a fairground ride, Kurtis longed to ask.

'Sorry for your loss,' a journalist said, shaking his hand.

It was the same journalist who had contacted him about Annie Campbell. They'd met a few years ago in the John Hewitt and, though it was far from his district, Kurtis hadn't felt comfortable at all. His reticence had prompted the journalist to comment 'Perhaps you're saving it all for your memoir.' Up to that moment Kurtis hadn't thought of writing about the disappearance; he'd viewed it as something that had happened to him rather than something that belonged to him.

Two weeks after his mother's funeral he was walking home from a couple of pints in the Longfellow when he saw Tyler for the first time in years. He would have recognised that swagger anywhere. 'That fella loves himself so much, he'd sit on his own knee' his mum used to say of him. As they passed, they nodded. Kurtis hoped he wasn't communicating the pirouette in his heart, and immediately looked down, pretending to be absorbed in the long line of russet leaves clinging to the kerb. The trees in the wind were making the sound of a roaring ocean. He realised twenty-four years had passed and Tyler was confident now in revisiting his old haunts. The last time he'd seen Tyler was the day before Annie Campbell went missing.

At home he opened a file on his laptop and began to tap out the words. He wrote with the squeal of Halloween fireworks outside, quickfire cracks of gunpowder and deep shuddering booms that would have raised even his mother from her grave, but the strength of his memories fazed it all out. At midnight he finally left the screen and went out to the street, enjoying the glitter in the sky and the ascension of sparks, the hint of cordite in the air.

The next morning he was up early for work. He'd been employed in the unclaimed packages department in Tomb

Street for years, but it never ceased to fascinate him, opening boxes and jiffy bags, wondering what he'd unearth next: drugs sent via the dark web, illicit polaroids, arcane healing powders, top secret legal documents, machetes, cancer tests ... Famously, he'd once unpacked a preserved monkey that had failed to reach a laboratory. And, on a few occasions, handguns. 'Sure, every day is Christmas in here' laughed his boss if there was ever a complaint or a murmur of dissent.

It was a never-ending pass the parcel. When Kurtis thought back to his childhood, he'd unwrapped gifts of toy tanks, soldiers and guns; his presents couldn't have been more militarised. He liked his job because of the unpredictability of it, but staff came and went because most of them couldn't hack the cameras trained on them. Having grown up in the Troubles he was grand about being watched – sure half the folk in his district had scouted for potential IRA bombers. Every few weeks at work the alarm bell would sound and the whole office – except for the one accused individual – would file outside while a search was conducted. As soon as Kurtis reentered the building the accused would be missing, fired for having slid drugs, money or a piece of bling into their bag.

In the first parcel of the morning, he found a bag of bright party pills. 'Hey, should we not keep these for our office Christmas party?' he joked, shaking them.

The Polish woman, Paulina, who sat opposite him, laughed. 'I'm up for a wild time if you are,' she said and it crossed his mind she was almost daring him.

At lunch, he sent a couple of emails off to local publishers, asking if they'd be interested in working with him on a memoir. He made sure to mention his connection with Annie Campbell as her name was the bait. There, he'd done it. Maybe the whole notion was ridiculous but he was tired of suppressing the past. His mum had had no truck with the past or the future; she'd strictly lived in the present. It wasn't fair that her advice to remain silent was still haunting him. Hers had been the generation to suppress emotions, whereas the new generation expressed things openly, relentlessly, purging themselves of all pain. If the old way was extreme, so was the new, and, perched in between them as he was, one didn't seem better than the other, but Kurtis was determined to use these times for his own benefit. It would be difficult to write about Annie, walking a tightrope between the real truth and the safe truth, but he'd leave all names out of it. He wouldn't implicate anyone.

At three o'clock he was opening his fiftieth package of the day when an email pinged back. It was Connswater Press asking him to meet up for a chat. 'I'm very interested' went the reply. A former classmate of his had scored a major hit with Connswater through a memoir of being a paperboy in Belfast during the 90s. Ok, so that story was more fun than his, but he was dancing around the idea that it could still do financially well and, besides, he was already thinking of selling his mother's house and buying his own place. As it was, even the walls seemed to echo his mother's words. 'You're a handless wee crater' the kitchen would tell him disapprovingly whenever he fixed his dinner.

He left work at four and, as the sun set, he headed back over the Albert Bridge to the east, past a line of maples as yellow as the Harland and Woolf cranes. He ambled as he went, kicking through the last of the leaf drifts. He even plucked a snowberry off a bush and squeezed it so the inside came out like a white milk tooth. He hadn't done that since he was a kid, but his mood was frivolous and carefree. The tawny light of the sun was coppering the beech trees.

Back at the house he looked at himself in the full-length mirror. He was still fairly lean, athletic. Of course, the face had a few lines and there were pouches below both corners of his lips as if he had wads of cotton wool there. His hair was dark brown even if his beard was peppering, and his eyebrows were well defined. He always clipped them and kept them neat. After Annie, everyone seemed to think there was some touch or taint of tragedy about him. Of course, he'd had a couple of girlfriends in his twenties but they'd never felt as right for him as Annie. When people asked why he hadn't found anyone he said 'It's just never happened for me.' At thirty, he'd moved back in with his mother who was suffering with her lungs and needed help with the heavy oxygen tanks. At the time she'd only been given five years to live, but made it to fourteen in the end. 'Thanks to you, son,' as she'd said in her last weeks. He'd done his familial duty.

It was time to live a little, so he phoned an old mate, Birchie, and arranged a party night with the lads.

'Aye, come over for a good blowout,' said Birchie. 'Time you got yourself a life.'

'Got yourself a life,' repeated Kurtis to himself when he rang off. Life wasn't something that just happened to you when you were born, it was something you had to go out and physically grab. To these guys it was like getting a job.

The next day the publisher Jan met him in the Linen Hall Library café and listened to his story. She was tiny, Glaswegian and had a reflective way of putting her head to one side and emitting a long, high 'ehhhm' like an acapella singer pitching a note, before telling him what she thought. She asked him to get underway immediately. The Annie Campbell case was still of huge public interest and personal perspectives on Troubles murders were in big demand.

'I'll work you really hard,' Jan warned him. 'And one thing ... you might think you're writing about Annie Campbell, but the story will always be about you, about your reaction and how it changed you. Are you ready for that?'

'I think so.'

He harboured a few worries about how Annie's family would react, but he was safe enough now that both her parents were dead, their health broken by grief, and her sister had moved to England. In any case, he'd loved Annie and wasn't going to reveal anything bad about her.

'I just hope I can write it well.'

'Don't you even think about that,' said Jan. 'Just write as much as you can and I'll edit it down. I know how to make even the weakest prose sing with the truth.'

That night he went to Birchie's flat over on the Ormeau. When he arrived Birchie had eyes wider than an owl's.

'Come on in, mucker,' Birchie said, giving him a warm hug.

Jordy and Owen were in the living room, sniffing cocaine off a plate through brightly coloured straws.

'Want a line?' asked Owen, passing him the plate.

'I don't take coke.' He was half-eyeing the door to leave. 'Never have.'

'Oh, go on, try a wee eyebrow, just to join us,' insisted Birchie, scraping a tiny trail of white powder especially for him.

It seemed rude to turn him down. Birchie explained the philosophy of their weekly blowouts. 'Life has its stresses. Sometimes you just need to burst a fuse, the way you burn a hole in your gutties when you run. See, some of us have too much energy and if we don't spunk it out, we might hurt someone.'

Kurtis sniffed the line of party dust and felt his eyelids lift open, his veins awaken.

'Fuck, that's you away, you'll be bodypopping all night big time,' laughed Jordy.

Jordy was married with five kids. Owen had a girlfriend as well as a kid he never saw to another woman, and Birchie had some sort of fuck buddy in tow. And he, Kurtis, had just come out of living long-term with his mother.

'Welcome to the brotherhood of the fucked up!' declared Owen, cracking open another bottle of Becks.

Kurtis knocked back a whiskey and again took the proffered plate. He had a sudden image of the collection plate being passed round his church.

'Go on there, boy!' urged Jordy, watching him sniff a full line only to end up sneezing. 'Fuck me, don't waste it. That's a tenner's worth a nostril!'

Kurtis was buzzing, the taste of metal in his mouth as he felt himself rise on the communal high. Was this 'getting a life'? It felt like it in the moment.

'Mega cool after all these years to be with you, bro,' he said, slapping Birchie's back.

'Only thing is in the morning you'll have a sore head like a Catholic got you,' warned Birchie, and he did.

It was such a hangover he never went back.

Over the next few weeks he wrote whenever he could after work and all weekend. Jan wanted to publish the book the following September to coincide with the twenty-fifth anniversary of Annie's disappearance. He finished the first draft by Christmas and knew himself it was a rush job.

'I want you to delve into the relationship with your mother,' pressed Jan, 'to really go deep into how and why she made you bottle the murder up.'

'Right. That's going to be hard.'

'I know you loved your mother,' said Jan, and the rest of the busy café was a blur as her words hit home. 'But don't protect her, don't spare her. It's part of the process.'

The process, the peace process, the grieving process, the writing process ... everything seemed to have its own allotted time. He stepped out into the cold air, walking past a child vandalising a frozen puddle with the heel of her shoe. Breathing in hurt his lungs. He watched a full-grown man take tiny baby steps out of fear of slipping on the ice.

An hour later he was back in the office with the rest of the packets team, back to unwrapping, pulling cellotape off, opening up, always keen to find out what was inside. Lately, he'd been noticing Paulina even more; how her hair was dyed an attractive shade of blonde, the way her upper lip slid up from her very white teeth when she smiled. He guessed she was in her mid-thirties. Two years working together and he'd never picked up on her charm. It seemed barely credible. It was like the sun had come into the room, shining only on her. He watched as she took a diamond engagement ring out of a parcel, then put it on her finger to model it for her co-workers.

'Sorry, just test driving it,' she grinned up at the camera and, just then, the way Kurtis was staring at her caught her eye.

It was a warm August evening on the precipice of twilight when Kurtis and Annie climbed over the gate into Knock cemetery.

'Christ,' said Annie, feeling the tear in her sweatshirt as it snagged on the spike of the railing. 'Mum'll kill me.'

'Mum'll kill me,' mimicked Kurtis in a high wimpy voice and Annie laughed.

'She'd kill me more if she knew I was here with you.'

They walked along the fir-lined path to an unkempt clearing full of old gravestones half-subsided into the ground, looking like a line of tilted dominoes on the verge of collapse. The grass was high and soft, as giving as a mattress. They had no other place to go and the weather that summer had been dry and beneficent; a summer for outdoor lovers. They'd lie there and touch each other, lost in themselves amongst the scurryings of mice and the churring of crickets and the last calls of birds as they settled in the trees. It didn't freak them out that they were surrounded by burial plots, as the bodies had lain there for centuries and the air was plump with the scent of honeysuckle and dandelion. As Annie pointed out, sure there were bones from old medieval churches under the streets that no one even knew about.

Tonight Kurtis was nervous as Annie had said she wanted to go all the way. He'd left the house with three condoms in his pocket. She wasn't his first, but he was hers, and the funny thing was the pressure of that made him even more nervous than if he was the virgin himself. They headed for their usual spot behind a tall monument and found a mound of twigs laid over it.

'Must have been an animal,' said Kurtis, sweeping the twigs away. Underneath was some sort of material half-buried in the soil.

'Wait.' Annie pulled a waterproof knapsack out of the earth. Its contents made a clunking sound. 'Buried treasure maybe ...'

Kurtis already guessed what it might be. He swiftly unzipped it, took out a bag of thick black polythene and ripped it open with his eye teeth. 'Shit,' he said, looking at the stash. The metal shone luminescently in the fading light.

'Fuck,' said Annie, reaching out.

'No.' He slapped her hand away. 'Don't touch.'

'What are we going to do with them?'

'Put them back where we found them,' said Kurtis, his hands losing control of the zip. The thought was coursing through him that at any second the guns' owner could return.

'Are you sure we shouldn't take them?' Annie asked. 'That way, no one can be shot.'

As he threw the twigs back over the bag, a bird trilled in a tree and there was a fissling sound. He had never been so scared, not even when he was chased by a gang of teens, nor when he was bullied at school, nor when he was a kid waking up from nightmares.

By April the grey lid of winter had lifted and the starlings were back on his yard roof browsing for insects in the moss of the blue slates. He'd finished the second draft and Jan said it was starting to take shape.

'Still some things to be teased out and untangled. Why do think she went back alone to the graveyard for the guns? Do you think it was just, as you say, to stop murders ... or do you think it could have been because it gave her a thrill to own something illicit, something valuable?'

'Maybe ...'

He guessed Jan was hinting that Annie would have derived a sense of power from taking the guns, as girls weren't allowed to play a part in the male world of the Troubles. He recalled how Annie had driven him home after leaving the graveyard. At the time he was thinking he'd missed out on sex, while Annie was still buzzing about their find. She'd given him a last passionate kiss in the car. He'd turned at the door, watched the car move away, her shadow waving at him and that was the last he or anyone else saw of her. He'd assumed she was going home.

She had never been found. No sign of the guns either. But her car was found outside Knock cemetery. Her disappearance was big news and all sorts of people came forward with information. More than one person had heard shots that night. Torrential rains had come the next day, hampering forensic tests in the area. Logically, he accepted she'd been killed by whoever came for the guns that night, but over the subsequent years he'd clung on to the dream that one day she'd come walking up to his front door. He couldn't forget the time in the graveyard he'd made her a ring from a buttercup and slipped it onto her engagement finger. There was a sense that his destiny was interrupted, so he kept waiting for her return.

Jan's voice broke through his memories. 'Columba McVeigh's mother was once asked "Would you never move house to try and move on?" and she answered –'

'No, because then there'll be nowhere for Columba to come home to,' finished Kurtis, understanding it perfectly as he'd kept his own home for Annie in his heart. 'I never knew before but the bullet that went through Annie that night went through me then and keeps going through me now.'

An odd mélange of compassion and acquisitiveness swept through Jan's eyes, letting him know he had to write those words.

As he walked back to the east, he could see the yellow of the gorse along the banks of the Lagan. It had been a mild wet winter and more yellow in the form of lichen lined the trees, illuminating their curves. Turning the corner onto My Lady's Road he bumped into Tyler. His first thought was that it had to be a coincidence before he realised Tyler was waiting for him.

'Hey, Kurtis, I've been meaning to catch up with you, ask you what you're up to these days,' Tyler opened.

'I'm grand. Working with Royal Mail, the usual.'

'I've been hearing you're writing. Is that right?'

He guessed what was coming, but tried to play it down. 'Oh, just writing a bit of a memoir for myself. No big deal.'

'I heard it was about Annie Campbell.'

Tyler looked at him squarely. He was still wearing a dark leather jacket, making it clear he'd never grown out of this uniform, never moved on, though his body had thickened and reddened. The jacket was tight on him as if he was a sausage about to burst its skin but, if anything, he looked even more threatening than in the old days.

'Uh, no. I mean I'll mention Annie's name in passing, but that's all.'

'I see,' said Tyler, eyes narrowing. 'We think you should drop it. Just remember, names don't want to be mentioned.'

There was a pause in which Kurtis could have reassured him but he couldn't stifle his indignation. What gave Tyler the right to intimidate him?

'I'm not going to mention names.'

'Don't mention anything. No one wants to think about that case. Time to move on instead of looking back.'

Aye, I know your way of moving on – agitating in Larne, threatening the staff who work at the Irish Sea border, thought Kurtis, but instead he said 'I promise you, I'm not going to make trouble for anyone.'

'You better not. Or there'll be trouble for you.'

'Ok, I'd better head on here,' said Kurtis, stepping round him.

As he walked away, he could hear Tyler's voice calling after him. 'Mind yourself, Kurtis.'

He scanned through his mind. How the fuck did Tyler know he was writing about Annie? Had he let it slip to Birchie and the lads the night of the party? Maybe Jan had spread it around, even though she knew the subject was inflammatory. Aye, it wouldn't open a can of worms, but a whole grave of worms. His heart was shaking as though all sentience had rushed up into his chest. Outside his house an Ulster flag had blown off the lamp post only to be pierced by the branches of a nearby tree. His hand had trouble inserting the key in the door.

He remembered how, a few days before Annie's disappearance, he'd said to Tyler that he took her to the old Knock cemetery because it was overgrown and there was never a soul about. There had been a glimmer of an idea in Tyler's eyes as he'd listened. Everyone knew Tyler stashed guns for the gunmen. Kurtis should never have told him.

He turned on his laptop and an excitement infused him that the subject of his memoir gripped people decades later. He knew now for sure that Tyler was guilty. Even if Tyler hadn't stumbled on Annie himself that summer night, he could reveal the names of the gunmen who had. Kurtis was going to write on to ensure that Tyler slept uneasily, that the whirrs of the crickets and the nuzzling snouts through the grass and the bird cries would echo in his head. What was that word Jan had used? Ah, yes, *unpack*. He'd unpack the story, he'd explain without mentioning any names how careless he'd been in telling people about his secret place, but it would still start the rumours, the whispermill of the east.

He couldn't sleep all night. He kept imagining his name appearing on a wall with an image of a crosshair beside it, and when he opened his eyes to the blinds, yellowed by the streetlights, he could almost visualise his name daubed across them. At four am he got up and went out to the damp backyard to check that the padlock was fixed to the hasp of the back door. Only two more hours, he told himself, and it would be light. Bravery always came in the light and he would be ready to write again.

On a bright May morning he hit the send button on his final draft to jan@connswaterpress.com and headed to work. White blossom framed the puddles and the blue of the sky bounced from the water. Above the mountains there was one cloud shaped like a stingray that slowly separated into white cartilaginous strands.

At work, a powerful smell of perfume filled the air. 'Oh no,' said Paulina as a broken perfume bottle fell out of the jiffy bag.

'That's some scent you're wearing today,' joked Kurtis.

'Ha, just for you, Kurtis,' she added, and there was something meaningful in her smile that prompted him to say, in spite of the other co-workers 'Maybe you should wear it out one night with me.'

'Maybe I should,' smiled Paulina.

A co-worker winked. 'Oy oy, what's going on here then?'

'Never you mind,' replied Kurtis, looking away from Paulina. Already, though, he'd decided to discreetly ask her for her number on their way out of the office.

A fresh trolley of parcels was arriving when he caught sight of himself in the windowpane. He noticed the lines down the side of his mouth, deep like a ventriloquist's dummy. He was forty-four while Paulina had fainter lines that shimmered in and out depending on the light. It had taken him many years to exorcise Annie's hold over him, but he'd done it now with the book. For sure, his mother and Annie had had the best of him, but he was ready for someone new. He kept his eyes on his reflection as the light changed and he watched his image strengthen.

LOVE IN THE TIME OF LOCKDOWN

There is a line in *Fleabag* where fifty-seven-year-old Kristin Scott Thomas's character turns down the beautiful Fleabag's come-on with 'I can't be arsed, darling.' It's almost unbelievable that Kristin is knocking back a woman twenty-four years younger! In her place, I'd have whisked her up to my hotel room within seconds.

I was entering year two of covid and homeworking from my desk which was next to the bed I hadn't shared with anyone in ages. In the past year the only physical contact I'd had was a drunken street kiss from a man called Des on his way back from the pub and an offer to come round to his any time. I liked him but had never acted on it. A few times I'd passed his flat and seen his profile with his mane of blond hair through the square window like he was on a postage stamp.

My first vaccine emboldened me to go round to Des's on a Sunday evening in March. I rapped on his window and he looked out at me, trying to place who I was, then waved me round to the front door. I waited ages, wondering why until finally he hobbled into the foyer wearing a moonboot. He was about three stone heavier and ten years older than the fond image I'd harboured from the summer.

'What happened?' I asked.

'Oh, I just tripped in the street,' he said, omitting any mention of alcohol.

Anyway, when I went into his flat it absolutely stank of dog. He brought me into the living room, shutting out his hyperactive pug who proceeded to hurl his body at the door. It was as if a jealous lover was pounding on it. I could hardly hear a word Des said so after a few minutes I left.

On the way out Des showed me his spare bedroom under the pretext of getting me to admire the clock on his wall. I was pretty sure he was showing me the bed for a reason, but although I've been with men with broken hearts I've never been with a man with a broken ankle and, even if he'd managed to haul his moonboot off, it would have been like being in bed with a Ming vase.

The trouble was the spring sun during lockdown was driving me insane. I was suffering from what's known as 'skin hunger', an extreme state of longing for intimacy. It was clear if I wanted the touch of some digits I'd have to go digital, and if I didn't want to be virtuous I'd have to go virtual. Everyone was going stir-crazy or 'boogaloo' as they call it in Belfast. Riots were breaking out and we were splitting out of our confines in the need to feel alive again.

And so, on I went to Tinder and set up my profile. I was fifty-one, but why go for my own age when I could get younger? For every cougar, there's an all-too-willing cub. However, I decided against going for the very young, in case I was spotted by a work colleague, and went for 35–50 instead. I didn't even bother writing a profile because I couldn't see the point of pretending to like Netflix or coffee or forest walks. The one hobby I loved was pubs, but pubs were still closed.

Most of my friends took sage for the menopause and wore magnets in their knickers, complaining of flushes and that their libido was dead, but as far as I was concerned it didn't make a difference if one minute I felt I was in the hot desert, the next in the Arctic – I was still just as sexual as ever. To me the menopause is just an excuse for lazy, undersexed women to do even less in bed.

Flicking through the profiles I began to consider my potential suitors. I avoided the men who posed in their sunglasses, the men who posed with children and definitely the men who posed with their pet dog. One thing I was starting to realise on Tinder was that if the only photo they give you is a headshot it means they're fat. Some men talked of looking for something serious and I instantly swiped left. What I've always looked for in life is an endless honeymoon. I'm an epicure, a hedonist, a bacchanalianist. People think I'm into no-feelings sex but I'm so romantic I find romance in the unromantic, meaning in the meaningless, feeling in the feelingless. Years ago there was this steamy sex film with Mickey Rourke and Kim Basinger called *9½ Weeks* but, to me, nine weeks counts as a long-term relationship. The truth is I don't enjoy the quotidian realness of a relationship, the arguments, the submission, the compromise. I'd far rather have one day of ideal over a year of real. Life is much too short for repetition.

At last I found the perfect profile; a selfie displaying his serious brown eyes and full lips with an unprepossessing grey wall behind. The naturalness of it. He was so real I knew he'd be ideal. I know that sounds like an oxymoron but life is full of contradictions and ambivalence. It was his words that made the greatest impression:

Looking for no strings sex. Any age, size, shape, race, religion. I don't have a type, just know what I like when I see it. Not looking for a relationship but doesn't have to be a one-time thing.

The delicious honesty of it. He didn't give his name, but his initials AM, so I guessed he was married, not that it mattered as that was up to his own conscience. The best thing was he was twelve years younger. What could I do but press like and he liked back, making us an instant match. Then we messaged back and forth. Obviously, I had to establish that he wasn't an axe murderer or stalker without actually asking if he was such. I'd just read about a woman murdered by her Tinder date and found in a forest. That wasn't quite the sort of forest walk I had in mind.

Our messaging felt easy, relaxed. I told AM about 'working' from home for the city council and he told me he fixed automatic gates and barriers all over Ireland.

> That's great you're good with your hands, lol, I said. Are you ok about breaking lockdown rules?
>
> *For you I want to be a lot closer than two metres if you know what I mean. [Wink emoji]*
>
> Great. Let's be rulebreakers. When are you free?
>
> *Mornings and nights. Is there anything in particular that excites you in bed or anything you'd like to try?*

The red light was flashing. I had to shut him down immediately or this was going to end up as cybersex and we'd never meet.

> I'm going to have to be honest here and say that talking is not my thing. In my experience those who talk about it rarely do it lol.
>
> *I would far rather practise than talk about it too. I'm really looking forward to meeting you. I better start doing sit ups to get myself in shape lol.*

The sit ups didn't bode well for his body shape, but, Christ, the trouble with online is that you start analysing every sentence for meaning. We were doing lols even when it wasn't funny, just to prove to the other we weren't raving mentalists. Clearly, an axe murderer would never do a lol as he'd take himself too seriously. Or she, though I'd never heard of a female axe murderer but presumably she exists if she does a bit of work on her biceps. Perhaps she'd use a light chainsaw. Years ago, when I first moved into my own house, my mum told me to keep a hammer under the bed in case of burglars, but when I brought a date back he caught sight of the hammer and was so petrified he scarpered!

AM contacted me every day and I have to admit it was touching to be asked 'How was your day?' No one had cared for me like that in years. I was beginning to appreciate the benefits of Tinder.

After two weeks of messaging, he arranged to come to mine for eight am on a weekday. It seemed fitting that AM was meeting me in the am, but I am not a morning person. I need more sleep than a sloth. During lockdown I wasn't getting up till nine and wandered round in a fugue till I finally slung on a jumper and opened my first work email. But for sex I'd do anything. When it comes to having larks, I'll always be up with the larks.

The day before meeting, he kept coming across as a strange mix of nerves and confidence.

I meant to ask, how would you like my privates to be presented?

On a silver salver I was thinking, and then he continued.

Hairy, trimmed or shaved?

I don't mind at all just as long as you feel comfortable. Natural is grand – unless we're going to film a porno movie.

I think I might be too nervous for filming a porno lol. There's still a chance you might scream and run away when you see me at the door lol.

Ha ha, there's always a chance you might turn and hightail it down the road yourself lol!

I will be a bundle of nerves for sure but the desire to get my hands on your naked body will stop me from running away. Oh and don't worry too much about makeup or anything. I'd be happy to see you whatever way you are comfortable with.

Makeup? He'd be lucky to have me showered by eight am.

The only thing I would ask is for you to wear a pair of panties. I'd very much like to peel them off you.

That's cool with me.

That night, it began to snow and the gusting wind kept blowing the flakes upwards. Under the street light they looked like the celebratory sparks of fireworks. I was so excited I kept waking every hour.

By the morning when his work van rolled up, snowflakes were drifting from the sky as desultorily as the petals from the cherry trees. I watched this giant of a man walk up to my front door. His face was exactly like his photo, only it was live and he smiled when he saw me.

We kissed and I could taste cigarette smoke.

'Want to come upstairs?' I asked.

'You bet I do,' he grinned. He spoke deep in the back of his throat in a countryish way.

Upstairs, we kissed some more. Then we got undressed and I let him unclip my bra and pull my pants down as he'd asked. He was built like a barrel-chested strongman – or an axe wielder, though I tried to suppress the thought. Almost instantly he was down on his knees on the hard floor worshipping my body, his hands roving all over my skin, his lips kissing me devoutly. I felt like a sex saint, a swami, a guru and it made the blood beat in my veins. He lifted me up so my feet were off the ground and set me on his knee, his fingers entering me, and I had a strange sensation of being a ventriloquist's dummy on his lap.

'You're really light,' he said, moving me onto the bed.

I'm a tall woman and not used to being lifted like a baby or a new bride, but for the first time in my life I felt tiny. His fingers were full of small nicks and frets. I asked about the tattoos on his upper arm and he told me they were Japanese symbols for evil, demons, vengeance, all the dark things.

Sometimes it's better not to be curious, but, luckily enough there was no symbol for murder.

He kissed me again with his soft full lips and I loved the drag of his goatee as he moved down my body. He buried his face in my flesh, his forehead turning a vivid pink, his eyes bloodshot. I could feel his tongue, lips and jaw moving laterally like a wolf shaking its prey. He kissed each bum cheek, then licked delicately down my perineum.

Through the open window, a seagull called out in longing.

'I have one thing to ask,' he said when he resurfaced and I felt some trepidation at what this stranger was going to suggest. 'Will you sit on my face?'

The relief of it, and then I rechecked 'Did you say sit?' worried I might have misheard.

'Yes,' he said, so I sat on him in a sixty-nine. I could verify that he'd definitely overtrimmed down there.

After a while, he got up and searched through his work clothes for a condom. Married, I thought, but I've always loved a man who takes sexual care. I watched him push back his foreskin and roll the condom on with shaking fingers. Under his penis, he had small balls, his sack almost like the pink mound of a woman, and I found it sweet.

He went on top, moving my legs so my ankles bounced lightly off his ribs, then pulling them up for deeper penetration so that my heels cracked off his clavicles. I could feel the scream in my hamstrings, but I didn't want to stop, I wanted to bend and stretch to his desire and my body had no say in it.

'D'you want to try any other positions?' he asked and I clambered on top, so that our stomachs slap-slap-slapped together in synchronicity. He let me fall on him to nestle my face in his neck as he jiggled and bumped and growled in his throat with the effort of coming. And it felt like I was being pulled by him into a wild joyous jig, the headboard banging to the beat of us, and I realised my neighbours who obeyed all covid laws to the letter would hear us through the walls. I made a mental note to avoid my doorstep for the next few days. When we moved apart, he still plucked and strummed at me, unable to leave me alone. I could feel his breath on mine, his face brushing mine, and I remembered hearing something beautiful once about how the Maoris touch noses to share the breath of life.

'You're my first ever redhead,' he said and I felt rarified and even honoured at devirginating him in the secret ways of us coppertops. I could see some rustiness under his fingernails and knew it was blood from inside me. He'd been rough, but I'd thought it unfair to complain when he was trying to delight me.

'The thing I most liked from your photo,' I told him, 'was your intense brown eyes.'

'They're brown on the outside and green on the inside,' he corrected me, making me laugh at his exactitude, 'but they were probably intense because I was trying to find the selfie button! I liked you because you're not like other women. They all have these rules like "No dicpics", "No assholes" or "No sex on a first date".'

'Really? That's not like men. Men don't issue any rules.'

'I'm not surprised. There was this woman who messaged me about arranging the wedding. We hadn't even met! I told her she was a psycho, so she reported me to Tinder.'

I laughed, but at the same time I remembered him joking in our messages that if he was ever kicked off Tinder it would be for an offensive profile. I'd slept with him, but I still didn't fully trust him.

We got dressed and went down to the hall to say goodbye. He still toyed with me a little, putting his hands in the back pockets of my jeans, then sliding his fingers into my front pockets teasingly, fooling around like a teenager, kissing my neck. I asked if he wanted tea but he didn't.

'I really want to do this again,' he murmured.

'Me too. We will.'

Because, if there's one thing I know, there's no such concept as 'no strings attached'. Even if the string is gossamer we will always bounce back to former lovers like a yo-yo.

He opened the front door, went out and closed it behind him, so I couldn't wave to him. I understood the need to avoid snoopers, but it struck me as a strangely private departure. I walked to the living room to watch him leave. He was just opening the van door when I saw a small dark-haired woman run up to him, a blur of elbows and knees, dressed in a light white dress even though flakes of snow were spitting from the sky. It happened so fast I couldn't believe it! Right outside my house she began to cuff him round the head. She was Megaera of the Greek Furies, all dark snaking hair flying across her face, lashing out now at him with her feet. Jesus Christ, it's the wife, I said to myself. AM looked shocked and didn't bother to defend himself.

Then she turned and looked directly at me. I leapt back from the window, but she was already shouting 'You leave him alone!'

She disappeared from view and I could hear her hammering on my door. 'I'll kill you if you ever see him again! Fucker!' she screeched.

I was petrified she'd break the door down. We hadn't been caught in flagrante delicto, in flagrante delicio, but we might as well have been. And I couldn't claim he'd come round to fix my gate because I didn't have one.

But oh no, she was banging on my window now, as if playing the lead role in some shoddy daytime soap. AM was pulling her away. All I could think was my neighbours, no, the whole street, would know I'd broken lockdown – and worse than that had broken a marriage. AM had grabbed hold of her arms and was talking to her quietly.

Then, the Fury calmed; within a minute everything had settled down. He drove off in his van and she drove off after him in her car. Separate. A passing dogwalker looked in at me through the window, big-eyed, wondering. I went upstairs and opened my Tinder account. Tinder was bombarding me with messages:

> We are currently vibing people and realise we know hardly anything about you ...

They weren't going to know anything about me either.

> Swipe surge in session. Someone superlikes you!

I couldn't care less if it was fucking Fleabag superliking me, I just wanted to get off the system.

> Join the party! [Eyes emoji]

I quickly deactivated my account. Five minutes later, I was virtuously opening my first work email of the day when I heard my neighbour open his front door. Just before he got into his car, he turned to look up at me through my bedroom window. I shrank back and then, to redeem myself in public, I picked up my mask, put it over my mouth and went back to work.

MOUNTAIN GODS

Shannon looked out of the taxi window as it weaved through Delhi. Families were resting on mattresses in the underpasses, their drying clothes festooned across the trees like coloured lanterns while, yards away, men were pissing against a barrier. In the dust myna birds fed on carrion.

Vehicles careered in and out of lanes, trucks trumpeting on every side. At the traffic lights a vendor danced through the cars carrying a crown of coconut slices on a tray, offering them up like a waiter, while a girl slinked in a double-jointed move through a hula hoop. It seemed the whole city was full of performers. Spotting their pale skin, the girl knocked on their window, but by the time they'd fumbled in their pockets the lights had turned green.

The taxi bobbed round a crammed tuk-tuk, one of its passengers hanging out like a stuntman. Shannon's seatbelt was broken, but she still held it across her chest in some vain hope it might protect her over the next six hours. She and her work colleagues, Marion and Aiveen, were on the first leg of their journey to the Himalayan foothills.

A roadside police depot was stark with government edicts: 'No Tolerance Zone – No Guns, No Smoking, No Drugs, No Drink'; 'Your support is critical as we fight crime and terrorism'. The taxi swung onto a motorway rising over the streets below. In the distance pink sandstone temples shimmered between the interstices of office blocks, and a billboard for The Electric Crematorium loomed huge.

Soon the motorway stretched out into the countryside past villages flanked by pampas grass. Women were spinning cotton while their men sold lemons and chilis from carts. In the fields farmhands threshed maize and the air was plumed with smoke from burning stubble, provoking a coughing fit from Aiveen even though the taxi windows were closed.

Shannon spotted men in white and women in black hijabs. Black and white like chess pieces.

'Must be a Muslim district.'

'Muslim villy-age,' confirmed the taxi driver, delighted to alight on the right English word.

'Oh, is that a Muslim village then? Right. Very good,' said Marion from the passenger seat, who kept passing repetition off as conversation.

They crossed the bridge over the wide, mud-coloured Ganges, pointing out the egrets and herons fishing in the shallows. Heading north they kept overtaking young guys on motorbikes ferrying multicoloured blankets stacked on the pillion.

The driver stopped off at some rough roadside café and held up his fingers to let them know how much time was allotted. A waiter was making ineffectual striations in the dirt with a broom. The toilets were rickety and, once inside, an alarming tide of urine was sluicing across the tiled floor. Things were even worse in the toilet cubicle where Shannon cried out in disgust at the urine seeping over her sandals, sending Aiveen and Marion into paroxysms of laughter.

Back in the car park Marion doused her hands and feet with tea tree oil. The men sitting at open air tables observed her public ablutions with unimpressed eyes.

'Want some tea tree?' Marion asked Shannon.

'You're grand. I have my own antibacterial.'

'But yours is all chemicals,' Marion replied, and Shannon felt guilty, reminding herself not to let anyone see it at the environmental conference.

They walked back to their taxi. Shannon smiled to see the sticker in the rear window that said 'This taxi respects women'.

Once they were on the road again the sky began to turn a pale blue and the sun grew stronger.

'Albie always planned to take me to India,' said Aiveen. 'He would have loved this.'

Her husband Albie had died in a car accident six years earlier, but she said she still talked to him every day and felt him by her side. Albie's pet name for her was Aivie, and nobody else ever called her that, but it was funny how the immigration officer in Delhi Airport had said Aivie instead of Aiveen.

'That one word told me in my soul it's right to be in India at this time,' she explained.

Shannon watched her brush away the ghost of a tear. The trio barely knew anything about each other even though they worked in the same offices at Belfast City Council. Aiveen was the oldest of the three at forty-nine, and whilst she carried a few extra pounds due to a gammy leg, she had vivacious blue eyes, a humorously malleable mouth, and pronounced herself ready for someone new. Since Albie, she'd had one brief relationship with a woman that hadn't worked out.

'But don't let that worry you,' she reassured them. 'Neither of you is my type.'

'What are you saying?' retorted Marion, mock-offended. 'Are Shannon and I not attractive enough for you?'

They laughed, glad of the relief. Eagles were circling around a rubbish dump that glowed effulgently in a field. A motorbike roared past, a woman riding sidesaddle in a sari behind her husband, a child perilously sandwiched in-between.

On the outskirts of the next village, a hoarding said 'Life should be great, not long'.

It was mid-afternoon when they turned towards Corbett National Park down a lane with cattle grids.

'Must be tiger grids,' joked Shannon.

As they got out of the taxi a peacock cried out from the canopy. The jungle felt like a breathing mouth of warmth and humidity. They walked through to the rustic-styled reception while a golf buggy transferred their suitcases to their lodges.

'Good timing,' the smiling manager informed them, pointing to a list of 'complementary ecological events' on a blackboard. 'You can still sign up for the riverside walk. It's leaving in fifteen minutes.'

Shannon and Marion leapt at the chance while Aiveen opted for nothing more strenuous than a lie down.

'But if you see an animal, the one thing you mustn't do is look it in the eye,' the manager warned, getting a kick out of scaring them.

Their guide, Bala, armed with a wooden stick, led them into the jungle. His English was limited but he was able to point out elephant damage to the bushes, a tiger's paw print in the earthen track, the berries foraged by bears, and the groove of a slithering snake. Shannon understood from Bala that at night the animals were allowed to own the forest.

The teak and eucalyptus trees began to thin out until they could see the dry riverbed through a clearing. They descended onto the flat plain, picking their way among the boulders. Halfway across, they heard a crack like a gun shot and the flapping of far-off wings.

'Gandhi gun,' explained Bala. 'Nothing killed.'

He lifted up a rock and pretended to hurl it against another before making chimp sounds.

'Ah, right,' Marion translated. 'That's what villagers do to scare the monkeys.'

Shannon borrowed his binoculars and looked across to the other side of the forest. No one could venture there except by jeep.

'Shh,' Bala warned Marion whose shoes kept slipping on the stones. 'Or tiger won't come.'

In the middle of the riverbed they sat down on a driftwood log peppered with woodworm. The sun was starting to converge on the treetops, the insects murmuring in a high tinnitus frequency. It wasn't long before a commotion sounded. Monkeys, parakeets and bulbuls cried out in warning as a deep vibrating 'ohmm' came from the foliage.

'Wait,' whispered Bala, sitting forward.

A tiger slinked out of the forest onto the rocks. The second it saw the three sitting on the log it stopped. Marion slowly raised her camera and clicked. It turned and crept under the shade of the bushes, head slung low, moving towards them. Shannon felt the fear of it and silently begged it to leave. The tiger paused, daring them to make a move, then disappeared into its side of the forest.

Bala jumped up, ecstatic.

'Yes! Tiger is great luck!'

Shannon could tell from his relief that he'd been scared too. They started traversing their way back across the riverbed. The sun was sinking behind the leaves, the sky tinctured with dusk.

At the edge of the forest Hindu music blasted out from a village, upbeat, more like a party song than a call to evening prayers. It was already dark under the canopy. A huge crashing sound came from the bushes making Shannon and Marion freeze.

'What's that?'

'Boars. Look!'

The wild boars rampaged past, released, reclaiming their territory and Shannon could feel their unfettered fever. Up ahead, the lights of the lodge reception shone through the trees.

That night while they sat out under the stars eating a meal served on banana leaves, Shannon felt a kinship every time she glanced across at Marion. The only other dinner guest was a woman from New Zealand.

'How come you got to see a tiger and all I got was a bloody elephant's bum?' she bemoaned. She had come to India as a respite from caring for her terminally ill parents. It occurred to Shannon that everyone came to India to escape.

'Look, I nearly swallowed a praying mantis!' said Aiveen, throwing it out with her wine onto the grass. 'Yuck! Jesus forgive me, that's the first time I've ever thrown out alcohol in my life.'

'It could be a new craze, like having a worm in your tequila,' joked Shannon. 'Everyone will want one!'

A few miles away in the village fireworks cracked through the night air and the manager explained it was wedding season. All Shannon could think about was Bala who'd gone back to his village. She kept dreaming about his dark skin and smooth chest in the v of his shirt, and the fear in him that afternoon. As they headed back to their lodges, the dogs in the village were howling.

The next morning another taxi came. The driver asked if they wanted to take the quicker, more winding way into the mountains or the straighter, slower route. Aiveen asked to go slow as she suffered from anxiety and the others agreed since they had the whole day to spare.

They passed Bala's village. It looked unkempt but picturesque: clay bricks drying in the sun, stacks of dung briquettes buzzing with flies, an open-air blacksmith's forge, a woman in a sari walking along the roadside carrying a bag of grain on her head.

'I opened up yesterday about my life,' said Aiveen. 'So who's next?'

'Me,' volunteered Marion.

She told them about the man she was seeing from London. They kept meeting up for weekends, taking turns to fly to each other's city, but whenever she suggested moving in together he always made excuses. She was beginning to reconcile herself to the fact he didn't want 'to lose his heart' to her, and going to India coincided perfectly with her need for a break.

'If he doesn't say he's missed me by the time I get home, I'm finishing with him. So that's me. Tragic!' she added with a grin.

In repose her face sometimes did look tragic, thought Shannon. Marion reminded her of a dispossessed Irish queen, some sort of Deirdre of the Sorrows, but when she was happy her face almost burst with it. There was no median with her expression; she was a person of extremes.

The air was turning fresher in the car with the ascent. Pine trees were clinging unfeasibly to the rocky hillsides.

'Are you sure this is the straight route?' Aiveen asked the taxi driver as the road began to zigzag. 'Accident Prone Area' said the signs. The driver beeped every time he approached a corner.

Marion managed to nod off in the front. That morning monkeys had woken her with thunderous leaps onto the aluminium roof of her lodge. She'd shouted at them as she'd left for breakfast only to come back to find they'd ripped up her talk about environmentalism on her verandah and pissed on it for good measure.

'I think I'm going to be sick,' mumbled Aiveen as they lurched higher towards the coloured chalets.

At last they swung over a hill overlooking the opal-shaped lake of Nainital and hurtled down towards it with the speed of a rollercoaster. Pink flamingo pedalos were locked up for the autumn and bobbed around on rusty chains. Streets were full of tourist shops with woollen jackets and traditional Sherpa hats. The gradient rose sharply again and the driver nosed his way into the narrow entrance of their hotel. Hotel Raj it was called.

'I assume the name's ironic,' commented Aiveen, as the staff in impeccably white tunics hurried out to greet them.

The environmental conference at Kingsford was packed at nine am. Delegates sat in the grounds of an ex-British hill estate overlooking Nainital. Green bunting, lit by the sunshine, fluttered in the breeze.

Before the opening speeches the host Shoba handed Shannon, Marion and Aiveen each a gold and red chrysanthemum, and applied a red powdery dot to their foreheads.

'Jesus, we look like we've been shot in the head,' Shannon muttered to the others.

Luckily, their event was on early. Marion led them in a panel discussion about greening and pedestrianising Belfast. As they left the stage they bowed their necks to receive linen scarves.

Later, lunch was served inside a wood-paneled dining room full of framed maps from the colonisers who'd built it. The speakers helped themselves to curries in silver salvers and gulab jamun bathed in sticky syrup covered in rose petals.

Shannon tried to slip out to the bathroom during the next talk, but opened the wrong door. Two Filipino servants were sitting on the stairs in the shadows while children bounced on a sofa in a living room. The servants looked startled and rose, but Shannon gesticulated that she'd stay till the event was over. When she looked out the window, however, she noticed various people, including Shoba, eyeing her in consternation. It was clear she'd made a real faux pas trespassing on the servants' quarters and drawing attention to the socially inequitable world Shoba was trying to hide. She exited with her head down at the next burst of applause.

The cloud rolled in and the temperature began to drop. All three shivered in their scarves and booked an early taxi back to the hotel. On the way Shannon noticed that almost every wall was enlivened by a Hindu shrine, as if the mountains were full of gods.

At eight they arrived at Snow View Hotel. Log fires had been lit on the terrace overlooking the hills. The delegates huddled together in their coats waiting for the fires to fully blaze but the sight of pink fairy lights hanging across the bar was warming. Shannon joined the queue behind a tall Indian wearing a woollen shawl. He ordered a red wine and turned courteously to Shannon.

'And what about you?'

'A Kingfisher, please.'

Just then, the electricity cut out, leaving the glow of the fires.

'Don't worry, it's always like that up here in the Himalayas,' he said.

The lights flickered on again.

'I like it. It keeps you on your toes,' grinned Shannon.

His name was Vikas, he was a barrister from Delhi and looked to be in his mid-forties. He had sweeping black hair with only the faintest few grey strands and a patrician tilt to his chin. There was something arrogant about him, but she assumed it was an act cultivated for the courtroom. He talked fondly of his three years studying law at London School of Economics where he'd had an English girlfriend.

They wandered over to the buffet.

'Indians eat so late,' said Shannon.

'I know. And when they go home their bellies are so full they can't make love, so men have to wake their wives early in the morning for sex – it causes all sorts of arguments, the divorce courts are full!'

'Our problem is we drink late. No one's perfect.'

'One thing I guarantee you, when you leave India you'll either love it or hate it.'

'I already love it.'

Vikas took the lid off a dish.

'Smells delicious. Try this chicken.'

'No thanks. I'm eating vegetarian in India as it's safer.'

'What? You're worried about a stomach bug, yet you walked into the forest to see a tiger?'

'You heard that?'

'Your fame has spread,' he smiled.

While they ate, some of the delegates got up to sing, but Vikas pursed his lips in disappointment.

'They should have hired girls from Nainital. There's a dance they do for the mountain ghosts. It's beautiful, erotic.'

As they watched Shoba sing Vikas confided that her family was royalty.

'She's a princess. Years ago I asked her to marry me but she turned me down. She was right to keep her freedom.'

It was on the tip of Shannon's tongue to ask if he'd kept his freedom too, but she already knew the answer.

Aiveen came up to her. 'Everyone keeps asking for an Irish song. So we'll do "Danny Boy", alright?'

'But I don't know the words,' protested Shannon. As usual she cursed her Protestant background for failing to teach her folk songs, but Aiveen was already pulling her onto the makeshift stage and roping Marion in too.

Marion and Aiveen sang with gusto while Shannon awkwardly chirped in on the few parts she recognised. Aiveen was in her element, interpolating local names where possible to charm the audience.

'From Nainital and down the mountain side,' she sung to gales of laughter.

Afterwards, Shannon was buttonholed by a girl wanting to talk about feminism. She could see Vikas out of the corner of her eye talking to Aiveen and tried to quell a little jab of unfeminist jealousy. It was a while before she made it back to Vikas and she was relieved to see him standing alone, waiting for her.

'Aiveen's great fun, isn't she?' she said.

'I don't think so. Maybe the things she says are funny but there's something dark in her, a little sad. I prefer you. You're *masti*, as we say in India – carefree. You have zing.'

'So do you.'

He held out a copy of *The Delhi Times*.

'I got this from the lobby for you. Just a piece I was reading this morning. Go on, I think you'll be interested.'

It was folded over at the headline: *Fifth death this year at Corbett Park*. A tracker had been mauled to death by a tiger two days ago.

Shannon scanned it. 'Jesus Christ!'

'You'll feel extra alive now,' Vikas chuckled.

'I already do right now with you.'

'Me too.' His eyes widened. 'I love your amber hair. Your skin.'

'If I was Indian what would be a good name for me?'

He thought for a second. 'Swarna. It means golden.'

'Swarna. I love it.'

'What about a name in English for me?'

She thought too. 'Alex.'

'Alex is excellent,' he agreed. 'Just like Alexander the Great. Call me ... Alex Sterling.' He struck a proud pose leavened by self-mockery. 'That's a strong name, isn't it?'

'Hello, Alex Sterling,' she grinned, but she wondered if the sterling implied an obsession with money.

'If I'm Alex Sterling you can be ... Swarna Bright.'

'She could tell from his eyes he wanted Swarna Bright, and the idea made her dizzy like she was on the edge of a precipice.

'So, Swarna, shall we leave together?'

They walked across the terrace, through the corridors and lobby and onto the road.

'Are you coming to the Raj?' asked Shannon.

'I think so. Or we could go to our apartment, but our servants are there.'

'Our?' she checked slyly, wanting him to disclose his marriage, but he wasn't to be caught.

'Oh, in India we always use "we" and "our" when we mean "I". It's collective thinking.'

'You have servants?'

'Of course. Like most of the people at the conference. You've been mixing with the elite caste.'

'Yes. I thought that.'

'But the thing is I'm different from them. Me, I want to do good with my money.'

Their voices sounded loud and drunken in the night air. They followed a winding road down a hill, deserted but for a teenage couple passing on a moped.

'Look at them. Young love is so beautiful,' said Vikas, and his words made Shannon hug his arm more tightly.

A string of lights from wooden houses looped across the hills.

'See? It's like Christmas here three hundred and sixty-five days of the year,' said Vikas happily. 'Have you ever felt it so still? Listen. It's like nature is watching us.'

He pulled her over and kissed her.

'What? Are you afraid to use your tongue? Another.'

He kissed her again, his tongue dipping deep before he stopped and stood back, almost in surprise at himself.

'This kind of thing never happens in Delhi – *never*. We're all so controlled there. You know I had to have an arranged marriage. I'm the eldest so I only had two choices – be in the police or be a lawyer. Some choice, huh?'

'Aren't you worried someone from Delhi will see us and tell your wife?'

'No. This is the Himalayas. You can do what you like here. For Indians this is like Shimla was to the British, it's our play park. It's like our Europe – anything goes.'

'Ah, that's why it's so special.'

'And it's more precious because it's a dream that will end. The mountains move here little by little every year and one day, maybe even tonight, there will be an earthquake and all these houses will fall down the mountain.'

They came to a fork in the road. Sagging electricity cables crackled, sending out a rocket of sparks.

'This way, I think,' he said, leading her down a lane with no lights, hardly wider than an alley.

She could smell the mildewed damp off the wall holding back the steep slope of cedars. The lane kept winding sharp right as though they were descending a helter-skelter.

He kissed her again and she could feel the tremors in his body.

'Have you ever made love under the trees?'

'Yes, but not now,' she said, stepping away from him. A sudden vision of him pulling her through a gap in the wall jolted her.

'No, no. You think I'd force you? Never. No way. I'd never hurt women or these mountains.'

To reassure her, he launched into a tale of a mountain god who kept trying to cut the head off a man but failing. It was only by seducing the man's wife that the god was able to sever his head. The story completely baffled her but she took it as a spiritual paean to love.

'You should see our mountains in Belfast,' she told him. 'Jonathan Swift saw the shape of a slumbering man in them who became the giant in Lilliput.'

'I'd love to see your mountains,' he said, wrapping his arms round her waist, lifting her high and swinging her round before lowering her so her lips fell onto his.

The trees were becoming taller, blocking out the light from Nainital. The lane was in so much darkness now that Vikas lit the way with the torchlight from his phone. After one more turn, the wall opened to reveal the lit-up entrance of the Hotel Raj and they walked up the stairs to her room. It felt cosy inside after the cold night air.

They started taking off their clothes. He unfurled his shawl with an airy flourish. She was surprised to see his sleeveless tunic underneath. He was so urbane yet traditional.

'I've two condoms,' she said, taking them out of her case.

'Two?' he scoffed. 'This is India. So many Indian men and you only brought two?'

''Fraid so. My economical packing technique has let me down.'

'We'd better use them wisely then.'

She was mesmerised by how black his cock and nipples were amid the pale honey of the rest of his skin. His hand reached out to the centre of her chest.

'You have warmth here,' he told her. 'The chakra is wide open.'

He licked her nipples and rolled his tongue down to her belly button before pausing to put the condom on. He eased her on top of him.

'Now sit back,' he instructed, making her arch away from him, pushing her hands back so they leant on his shinbones. 'Breathe with me.'

He breathed more and more excitedly. 'Can you come?' he asked, and when she lowered her hand to touch herself, he pulled it aside. 'No. You use your fingers too much in the west, don't be selfish. Make me come with your own energy. You don't need hands.' He pointed to where her power was. 'Sex is all through your chakras from your head to your pussy.'

'Thanks, guru,' she grinned.

'Go on, work. Concentrate.'

'You're very demanding, Vikas.'

'Haven't you ever been with a barrister in bed? We're all like this. And you can call me Viki.'

'I can't call you Viki,' she laughed. 'It's like a girl's name.'

'Right,' he said with a smile, bucking her violently on his hips. 'Just for that I'm going to make sure you can't walk tomorrow.'

'No, let's try something else.' She moved across the bed to a different angle.

'No, it's better if you face me. We're not animals.'

She felt him run his hands over her, digging deep into her arms, then gliding down between her fingers. She thought of the jungle and the pulse of it and the crashing and the cries. It was still within her, even inside this quiet room in the mountains.

She sucked him for a bit and he writhed before sighing 'I can't. And I wish I could. I shouldn't have drunk so much.'

'It's ok,' she soothed.

'I wish I was free like you,' he lamented. 'In India we can't have a private life. We're only allowed a family life.' A light stutter came from the windowpane. 'Rain. It's not only on the outside but the inside ...' Vikas raised himself up, smoothing back his hair. 'I won't sleep all night now. Have you any cigarettes?'

'No, sorry, I don't smoke.'

'Pity. When I can't come it's the only thing that helps me sleep.' He got out of bed and started pulling on his clothes. 'If I could stay longer I'd show you my land, my walnut trees. It's glorious, but I have to drive back to Delhi early.'

She walked him to the door and he bowed to her. 'You see these hands together? In Hindu one hand is god and the other is man. But now, this hand is Alex and this one is Swarna.'

Shannon bowed back to him. 'To Alex and Swarna. I'll never forget you.'

'Oh, well, thanks very much for that,' he said ironically. 'I was going to ask you for your number. Maybe we can meet up again when I'm in Europe.'

She pressed it into his phone. One last kiss and he left.

The following morning at six thirty Shannon hurried out to join Aiveen and Marion in the taxi.

'So how was it with the Roman consul?' asked Aiveen, making Shannon smile to think of Vikas's imperial demeanor and his shawl.

'It was great.'

'How come you got him and I didn't? I was chatting away to him too last night, entertaining him when you were off with other people,' said Aiveen. 'What am I, your fluffer?'

The taxi twisted its way wildly up the deserted, corkscrewing road towards the hilltop. Tree roots protruded on the verge of a landslide.

'You never told us your story, Shannon,' said Marion.

'There's nothing much to say. Sure there were men I had relationships with, but I was never married. I'm not like you two, I don't want to live with a man.'

The sun was edging its rays over the hill but the driver closed the windows as the air was getting icier.

'Is that it?' Aiveen asked.

'There was never one great love in my life,' said Shannon, not knowing if it was true or when to start or end her story. 'I think my story is about freedom,' she said, 'and moments,' but as she spoke, the words hit the air and froze. All she could visualise was Vikas with his wife and kids in the shadows next to him. The word *masti* crept back to her mind as did the image of the slinking body of a tiger heading back into the leaves.

The route climbed higher cutting through swathes of forested rock. On the low walls circumferencing the road small monkeys fought, frolicked and fornicated. Bells rang from an ashram. Goats were tethered outside a small grocery kiosk.

Finally, they could see the breathtaking triangles of white snow peaks jutting up above the misty green hills. It felt like being on the apex of the world but the taxi driver who was anglophonically-challenged indicated that Mount Everest was far away on the other side of the range. They arrived at the highest view point, pulling in behind a couple of tour buses.

'Eight o'clops,' said the taxi driver, letting them know what time he was leaving.

Brass telescopes lined the roadside. Photographers were snapping Indian tourists adorned in crimson velvet mountain dress and posing against the grey cliffside. Nearby, a man with eyes as sharp as a civet kept harassing them to use the telescopes. When they wouldn't take up his offer he spat out brown betel juice in disappointment.

They stood and stared across at the geometric planes of white under the blue morning sky. Shannon couldn't help thinking of the quote from the poet Sappho: 'What cannot be said will be wept.' They felt the vastness of the Himalayas outweighing their childhood images, and the privilege of being a flesh and blood witness. They sucked in air that was so cold and pure it felt healing.

'Stunning,' said Aiveen, brushing her hand against her eye.

THE SUN THROUGH THE SMOKE

In the afternoon Ray walks round to Avoniel Band Hall to survey the damage. The door is scorched, the paint blackened into bubbles. Under his feet, the concrete is melted and pock-marked, undulating like the surface of the moon. 'Any idea who did it?' he asks the bar manager.

'No one's said a word, but it could be Bryson Allen. Sure we barred him last week.'

Ray flips the notion over in his mind and heads back towards the Castlereagh Road. He can see the mountains in the distance and the smoke from a gorse fire high on Cave Hill curling in the wind with its own calligraphy. The dove grey clouds seem to be gathering, making him shiver a little. In his office he opens his laptop and rereads the article about the widow of a famous loyalist selling her husband's archives at a Dublin auction house. Eighteen thousand, marvels Ray. He remembers the diaries he used to keep, imagining how a Troubles museum would snap the hand off him now for such secrets. He'd sat at the table with Bill Clinton too, and although it might not have been as sensational as Bill's adventure under a table, details of the peace process were highly collectable. Still, he'd thrown those diaries out long ago because they revealed too much.

The rain has started to slam down on the streets. He looks out to the hills again, but this time they're clothed in a white pall and almost invisible, save for a low grey blur. At this rate he'll be working in this office till he's sixty-five. Sometimes he dreams of going somewhere hot like Spain for a month to write a thriller based on his experiences. He's scrolled through all those websites with writers boasting of a novel within a month, so he can't think it would be that hard to achieve. The pale sandstone of the church is turning dark in the rain.

Joanne, who works on reception, knocks on his door. 'There's someone here to see you about a plumbing course,' she tells him crisply and he moves back into work mode.

At home he's been waiting days for a dry evening to mow the lawn. A bright blue is shearing its way through the clouds but the lush grass is still wet.

'There you go, lucky Ray, saved by the rain again,' says his wife Ann, making him laugh.

Instead, he opens the sideboard and takes out the box entrusted to him by Johnny Allen two years ago, just before he died of cancer. Johnny Allen was one of those men who had let the ghosts into his mind, split up with his wife and taken to the tranqs and diazies. Johnny had spent the rest of his life estranged from his son Bryson thanks to the invisible peaceline erected by his wife between her house and his.

'I want you to do something for me – flog these and pass the cash on to Bryson,' Johnny had fluted hopefully as he'd dropped the box off. His face was radish-red from a reaction to the chemo.

'Yeah, sure. The old family heirlooms, eh?' Ray had joked at the time. 'Two bullets and a Glock.'

But it seems Johnny was cleverer than Ray had thought and there's a market for old memorabilia and there's treasure in trauma. Ray pulls out a box of matches bearing the Red Hand insignia and the words 'Springfield Road 1970'. It's perfectly preserved as if Johnny had bought it only yesterday to raise funds for Protestants burnt out of the Springfield Road. An uncomfortable feeling comes over Ray. Going back to the past is like letting an alley cat into your home. He has to keep the coffin lid closed, the back door locked, the memory box chained; keep alert at all times to avoid ending up a shriveled wreck like Johnny. He sets the matches aside, calculating they could be worth up to a thousand pounds alone, and kicks the box of letters into the space next to the sofa for later perusal.

In the bathroom he surveys his face in the mirror. He's always thought he looks good for sixty but his bald head is like an egg tapped with a tea spoon, leaving the cracks of crisscrossed lines on his forehead. He still has strong shoulders despite his habit of hiding them. Back in the 70s his trainer had been obsessed by Mossad and had instructed him on how to make himself small. Average.

'I'll teach you how to walk into a pub, then walk back in three hours later so even the barmaid doesn't recognise you,' the trainer had promised.

Christ, he thinks, realising what the matches have reignited. He shakes his head and runs the taps, dousing his face. He joins Ann down in the kitchen, her quick hands slicing the little skeins of fat from the pork. She's faring well for her age too, but when you look in closely, her skin shivers a little when she talks, like wind flaws on the surface of a puddle, and there are laughter lines spoking around her eyes. While she might be heavier round the middle these days, he finds it suits her. It makes her grounded, gives her a gravity, a kind of emotional ballast that centres him. During the Troubles, girls flocked to him, longing to be touched by the hands that held the gun, but not once had he ever cheated on Ann because he knew he'd unravel without her. And Ann has had her own fair share of troubles. It was their rule, their code to say little throughout all her illnesses; an early hysterectomy followed by removal of her appendix and gallbladder. She sometimes joked that there was so little left inside her if you shook her she'd rattle.

'There's the sun out at last,' says Ann, nodding at the light splicing through the garden.

'I'll get to that grass tomorrow, well.'

Her brown eyes run over the uneasiness in him. 'Something wrong, Ray?'

'No, grand. Just thinking about Johnny's son, Bryson. That kid's always in trouble.'

'Like father, like son,' Ann says lightly.

He heads out into the garden to hang the washing on the line. The sky is pure blue after all that rain with only the faintest fishbone trace of cloud. He muses how the endless seesaw of the skies proves that life can always turn for the good. A huge low moon is tinged orange from the sunset, its dark spot reminding Ray of the birthmark on his back. *Well, I always was a loon, a right mooncat*, he chuckles to himself. As he takes the basket indoors there is still a faint burning scent in the breeze.

That night he wakes up rolling onto his face as if turning away from a bullet. His chest is slicked with sweat, making him yank off the duvet. He wonders if the heat is coming from Ann who sleeps like a furnace, but when he pats the small valley of bed between them he finds it cool. Images are running pell-mell through his mind of putting on his Celtic top and his St Christopher to go undercover, of standing in a huge crowd of mourners on the Falls, of watching the pallbearers carry the tricoloured coffin along the road, of stopping outside the pallbearer's house and pulling out a gun. The words of his trainer filter back to him. 'What do you do if the target is sitting there holding his baby? Or what if you go in and it's the wrong man? I'll train you up as well as I can, but until you're in that split second, eye-to-eye, you'll never know what you'll do. On another day, another time, in the exact same situation, your decision will be different.'

As the years ticked past he learnt better ways to infiltrate, and took on a job as a sales rep travelling round the pubs from Ballymena to Belfast. The sales company was Catholic and his West Belfast clients assumed he was one too. He called himself Raymie from Whiteabbey and, if questioned, he let on he was a mucker of a famous republican drinker called Big Jim. He'd be laughing away, having the craic, while running through his own personal inventory: is the door caged, is it cameraed up, who sits where, what's the barman's name ...? And he was wary of everyone, even those on his own side, because his trainer had told him the story of the great Ulster warrior Congal Claen who was slain by some half-wit wandering across the battlefield.

He turns the tourniquet tight round his memories and returns to images of childhood sunshine, of his mother slapping the buttery tanning cream on his skin, attempting to coax his gingery hue into a golden batter. Some pasts are better than others and it makes him smile to think of a kite's handle skittering in his hands. He feels safe there, and before he knows it he's out of his dreams and the morning sun has slid into the fissures between the slats.

At lunchtime he leaves his office and threads his way through the back streets in the treacling sun. A pigeon scutters out of his way, its wings making a high whistling sound of alarm. He's made some phone calls about Bryson and found out he's moved his pitch from the band hall to the bonfire. It's high time Ray approached the lad about the possibility of making money from Johnny's papers.

The tower of pallets never ceases to impress him. Five days to go till bonfire night and it's already like the comb of a giant beehive buzzing with children. He stands for a while, scoping the scene, taking in all the details. A few teenagers are sitting on a discarded leather sofa overlooking the bonfire, but there's no sign of Bryson. They look up at him combatively and he repays their hostility with a cheery 'Alright, lads?' back to being non-threatening friendly Raymie of the old days instead of cool-eyed Ray.

'The boney's looking great,' he says to allay their suspicions.

Just then he spots Bryson come round the corner, strutting cockily in his white trainers as if kicking the air. The sides of his head are shaved, the hair on top gelled upwards like a scrubbing brush. Ray takes in the pouched pockets of his hoodie.

'So, lads,' he continues, 'I work for a community organisation offering free training courses if any of yous are interested.'

They scowl at him, pretending their faces are screwed up from the sun. He knows perfectly well they want him to go in order to do their deal in peace, but he pulls out some business cards from his wallet, making sure they see the crisp notes fresh from the till. Teenagers only seem to respect money these days, though it strikes him with a pang that if these young ceasefire soldiers knew what he'd done they'd worship at his feet. Outside the old guard nobody knows him, and he traded fame long ago for a quiet anonymity and what they call 'credibility'.

Bryson pockets a business card without looking at it.

'By the way I knew your da very well,' Ray says. 'He was a good man.'

Bryson nods, a cross between acknowledgement and a sneer. He scratches his slender arm dark with tattoos, like he's itching to hit Ray.

'I see you're a man of few words, just like Johnny,' grins Ray. 'Anyway, see yous around, lads.'

He can hear some low laughs behind him and ignores them. He consoles himself that at least Bryson didn't chuck his card away. He looks up at the sky and it seems promising for his lawn-cutting mission. A heat haze the colour of cloudy cider is hovering above the dark green mountains while, over to the east, he can spot plumes of rising smoke, perhaps from a bonfire. A helicopter is buzzing around the smoke like a wasp drawn to its scent.

As soon as he gets home at six he mows the short strips of lawn front and back, blades whirring the grass stalks into the air, tossing up that delicious dewy scent. Ann makes him chicken with the thick cut chips he loves, huge and yellow like the girders of Harland and Wolff. The vinegar gnarls his lips just the way he likes it.

Afterwards he takes Johnny's papers upstairs and starts leafing through them. Most of the letters are government missives inviting Johnny to talks with top republicans. Ray recalls those early bitter meetings face-to-face with his enemies where he literally had to sit on his hands to stop himself throwing a punch. Underneath is a yellowed, frayed invitation to Harvard University. Ray had joined him on that trip and he can still barely believe it; imagine a pair of Belfast backstreet boys explaining loyalism, swapping the machine gun for the microphone in those hallowed Harvard halls. Nobody could ever take the memories away from him.

He pulls out a green jotter full of Johnny's crow's-claw writing. He reads the first paragraph, accustoming himself to the spikes and loops of the lettering and the odd orthography. Johnny was no writer, but it seems to be an attempt at a memoir:

> There were four in my unit – me, Ray, Kenny, Clarke. How did we never get charged? We were the 'no-statement men'. That meant when we were arrested we never ever gave a statement to the police. We trusted each other like brothers ...

Ray sits reading, transfixed. He can't believe he's kept this evidence in his own house over the past two years. Why hadn't he checked it before? The last time he was raided by the police was years ago, but even so he needs to be careful.

One element to success omitted from Johnny's account was luck. Ray remembers the four of them in the car on a wintry, sleet-spitting night being stopped by the army. If the soldiers had searched under the seats they'd have found machine guns, but the corporal waved them on. He reads on until dusk darkens the text. When he looks out to the house opposite he can see a white blouse hanging on the back of a door, a hovering headless ghost. The street lights flicker into life as pink as rats' eyes. He hears Ann's footsteps on the stairs and moves back to his papers with a semblance of guilt. But he has nothing to be guilty about. All his life he's taken the Martin McGuinness line of accepting corporate liability for causing hurt and pain but there's no way he'll ever accept personal liability for a war he didn't start.

'You've been up here hours. Anything of value?' she asks, handing him a cup of tea.

'Oh, I don't know if it's worth much. Just a walk down memory lane.'

'Or down a dark alley if I know you lads,' jokes Ann. 'Come and watch Gogglebox when you're done.'

'Aye, in a min.'

There's no doubt in his mind Johnny's testimony will garner tens of thousands, but the issue is it will send him to prison for the rest of his life. He walks over to the skirting board. He kicks it gently and it makes a reassuring hollow sound. The gun nook he's always called it in his mind; he'll stash the jotter next to his gun from now on. He closes the curtains. Down in the street one of his neighbours is standing with his fingers across his lips, sucking on a cigarette in his doorway. It's as if he's telling Ray to hush.

The following day the wind is blowing a hooley. Ray looks out of his office window and sees the weeds along the kerb ripple flatly like reeds in a river. He can't drive the past out of his head. It's inside there now, residing in the membranes, synapses and neurons in the same way that cancer becomes part of you, mutating every cell. Outside, the shutters rattle in their rails. It occurs to him that the only way he can sell Johnny's jotter is if he goes through it and cuts out the names of the cell members. *Or redact it*, he tells himself, proudly pinpointing the right word. It took him to visit Harvard to realise that a facility with fine words is acquired and not innate. He tries to go back to work but his thoughts are blindsiding him. If Johnny was prepared to sacrifice his own name in order to help Bryson, it's Ray's responsibility to make it happen. Yet it will surely harm Bryson to know the truth and, besides, Ray has to consider the effects of Johnny's words on the victims' families. Not that the combatants he killed were ever true victims in his eyes, but some people view them as such.

'You don't seem quite with it today,' says Joanne, noticing the glaze in his eyes.

'I haven't been "with it" since I wore velvet ankle boots in the 80s,' he laughs, making fun of her phrase, and tries to refocus. He rings up some course providers to check availability.

An hour later he's about to leave the office when he spots Bryson, buffeted by the wind outside, ringing the buzzer. The boy looks smaller away from his streets, less edgy, and he stands at the door like a shy animal on the verge of bolting.

'You got a minute?'

'Yeah, yeah, no problem,' Ray says, ushering him in. He has a strange sensation that he's conjured up Bryson by thinking about Johnny. 'How can I help you?'

'I'm after a course. You said you run courses.'

'I don't run them but I can set one up for you. We fund courses to train plumbers, electricians, joiners –'

'I want a first aid course. Can you set that up?'

'Yeah, sure. First aid's great. It's a transferable skill and will help you in whatever career you –'

Bryson cuts across him spikily. 'Yeah, whatever. All I want is the first aid course. Nothing else.'

'That's fine. Just give me your number and I'll get back to you.'

'Sound.' He looks pleased but doesn't want to admit it.

'I'm about to lock up here. Do you want me to run you home?'

'Nah. Got my own wheels. Catch you,' he says and he's already gone, leaving the faint scent of nerves and hair gel in the air behind him.

Ray smiles to himself, chuffed, but lapses into wondering if the only reason Bryson wants the course is to save the lives of teenagers who ingest his drugs. But what right has Ray to cast judgment? He and Johnny had already been trained to kill by the time they were Bryson's age. By seventeen they'd done their first hit. Different times, different crimes, he tells himself.

He locks the door behind him and steps out into the street to pull down the shutters. A beer can is rolling down the pavement, chattering in the wind. The wind slaps his coat against his back almost as if he's being patted in congratulations. At least he's helping Johnny's son. Hasn't he made good on his promise enough without having to sell Johnny's papers too? He gets into his car and drives home under a sky that is shale-grey except for a small porthole of weak sunshine. The paramilitary flags are outstretched like beating wings, a church steeple piercing the cloud like a closed umbrella, and his wheels crunch over torn-off branches and twigs in the shape of wishbones. The seagulls are wheeling above and swooping. They seem to be crying out to him, urging him to act. He keeps hearing the trainer's voice in his head. 'The newspapers will call you cowards for what you do but let me ask you this – isn't shooting a man in the back of the head more humane than giving him five or six seconds of terrible fear?' When he reaches his house the red buds shivering on the fuchsia hedge remind him of freshly shed drops of blood.

'Oh, great, you're back early!' calls out Ann, hearing him open the front door.

'I just have to sort something,' he tells her, hurrying up the stairs.

She heads back into the kitchen, knowing better than to ask, and he's grateful for it as he has been a million times in his life. He opens up the skirting board. Waiting to decide has been killing him these past days. The jotter looks so innocent, just like a school book and, as he flips one last time through the childish handwriting, he doesn't want to eradicate another man's voice, but neither does he want to immortalise his friend as a murderer. What people never understand is that it was a dirty stinking war and they were only kids when they joined. An uncle of Johnny was murdered in the early days, tainting Johnny's blood with the pure fire of vengeance.

He picks up the matchbox with the jotter and walks back down the stairs, so caught up in his thoughts he's barely aware of moving. This is what happens when you let the past in; the present becomes a dream through which you sleepwalk. He hardens his mind and goes out to the garage where he keeps the canister for his lawnmower. He walks into the garden, the wind billowing out his jacket, and finds a sheltered spot by the wall. He throws the jotter onto the ground, douses it in petrol and kneels.

'Sorry, Johnny,' he says as he tries to light the match head against the striking surface. It won't take. Not so much as a spark, and it seems that the fifty years of damp has eroded its force. The matchstick breaks in the vice of his thumb and forefinger and he pulls out another. He keeps striking until the match begins to spark. With each strike an image hits him; the time he laid his first bomb, hoping it would kill; the time he hurried up behind the pallbearer in his damp slippery yard and shot him in the back of the head; the time he smiled in the pub at the men he knew would be shot; the time he and Johnny ran into a living room to see the target standing by the sofa nursing his baby in his arms and how he fired into the man's face while Johnny shouted 'No!' and watching, as the man's legs jerked out, the baby fall onto the floor. And oh god, that thud of the baby's head!

The match finally lights, the fire blooming up and taking hold of the jotter. His stomach is knotted and snarled, heat raging through the branches of his lungs.

'Sorry,' he says to Johnny for giving him such nightmares and for prospering all these years while Johnny faded and failed into a grey worn-out shell of himself.

The jotter curls and twists as if an invisible monster is taking great bites out of its spine. The smell of burning is beneath him and he wonders if the burning will ever leave him or ever leave these streets. He straightens up, his coat whipping against his back as the wind rasps around him. He has a sudden sense that the heavens are exhaling with him. When he looks up, the dark clouds are nimbed with white and a blue is breaking through.

McCrory's Millionaire

'Are you sure he's a millionaire?' Mum asks, while my dad rubs his hands together excitedly in the background like a gleeful Protestant minister.

'We'll have to crack open the good glassware,' he says.

'Aye, for we could be on the hog's back with this new man.'

It's rare for Mum and Dad to be impressed by me. I've just returned to their home in Dundrum after two years teaching English in Poland. Each time I Zoomed them they witnessed my dilapidated Warsaw flat, which was as rough as Calamity Jane's cabin. I've had what they call 'earning disabilities' for a long time, but in Warsaw I met a Mancunian by the name of Tony who owns a real estate company. What I've omitted to tell my parents is he has a Polish girlfriend called Kasia and a secondary relationship with the English woman who runs his office. I don't want to spoil their excitement – or is it just that I'm enjoying boasting for once? The word 'millionaire' has blown their hair back.

'Right, we'd better redd the place up for this Tony fella,' says Mum. 'Look what you've done to the cushions!' she shrieks, beating them back into shape. Whenever she has guests the house turns into a stately home – you can't touch a thing, let alone sit on the soft furnishings. You're expected to float around mid-air.

'I have to forewarn you,' I tell her. 'He's fifty-three.'

'Well there's nothing wrong with a mature outlook.'

'It's the mature look is the problem. Still, he's pretty fit on it.'

Before I know it, she's on the phone, crowing to the family about Tony.

'He works in the property market in the EU,' I can hear her say. 'He's in his forties, extremely good looking too. They've been together all year, Cara says.'

'That was some lies you gave it there, Mum,' I say afterwards.

'Sure I have to keep the side up. Everyone else is bumming and blowing about their kids.'

It's a fair point – the McCrorys in particular are always giving it large. I've already overheard Mum pretending I've been to interviews in London. Talking of interviews, that's how I met Tony. I'd applied for a job as a sub-editor on his monthly property magazine. I didn't get it, but made it through to the second interview, and to several more private meetings after that, if you get my drift. He took me out to restaurants and I enjoyed a bit of the high life, but then the teaching year ended in June and I went back to Dundrum.

I wasn't expecting to see him again until today's phone call telling me he was in Belfast sussing out some property and he'd love to drive out tomorrow at twelve and meet me at my parents'. It was the way he arranged it all without me having hardly any say. I guess that's why he is a millionaire and I am, as Dad would call it, living off the bones of my arse.

But it does get me wondering; why does he want to meet up with me again? Has he split up with Kasia? Is he planning to go out with me long-term? I can't think it's just bricks and mortar that's brought him to Belfast; surely it has to be flesh and blood.

'I'll get the wine in,' says Dad. 'Does he drink red or white?'

'He doesn't drink.'

Dad's mouth goldfishes. 'He doesn't drink?'

'Not a drop. How do you think he got to be a millionaire?'

'Would he not drink low alcohol?' Dad is almost pleading here.

It's just as well Tony doesn't drink. Every man I've ever brought to the house has been drunk under the table by my dad. He calls it hospitality, but it's almost like he's testing them, like it's an arm wrestle to see if they're genetically fit enough to join the McCrory clan.

The next morning, after a dawn assault of hoovering, dusting, windolening, bleaching, polishing and cushion-plumping, the house is ready to accommodate a millionaire. Dad returns from Tesco's with a boatload of food, more than you could legally cross the Irish Sea border with. In two flicks of a lamb's tail, Mum has Dad topping and tailing the beans and me trimming the fat from the fatted calf. Fortunately, Tony is not a vegetarian, which would be an added insult after his teatotalitarianism.

'Cara, he'll not be able to resist you after this dessert,' says Mum, whipping up a soufflé.

'Look, I hate to disappoint you but this is not a Jane Austen novel.'

'You know how he's looking for property in the area? Would he not set you up in a wee flat?'

'God sake, Mum. Are you asking me to be some sort of concubine?'

'Well, you have to think practically these days.'

'You won't get anywhere living off His Majesty's Benevolent Fund,' chips in Dad.

The two of them would happily pack me off to Tony's international seraglio, but I have my own plans. I head upstairs and fire up the laptop. I Google 'teaching jobs abroad', dreaming of another swift escape, but hesitate and type 'career in journalism' instead. I've got to do something to stop the drifting. I've even started sending satirical think pieces out to newspapers, though sometimes I think the only way I'll get a move on with life is if I'm strapped into a battery-powered exoskeleton.

A text comes through from Tony. 'Leaving early. See you at eleven.'

Now, here is a man who does not let anything drift.

The news sends the kitchen into a frenzy. There is frantic whisking, chopping, microwave dinging, oven timer ringing, heat, smoke and more condensation than a Swedish sauna.

Tony's arrival is so important to Mum she makes Dad change into his good black church shoes that pinch his toes. Dad can barely contain his excitement either as the closest he's ever been to a million is winning three numbers out of six on his lotto ticket.

'What are you going to wear, Cara?' Mum asks.

I don't think it's that important considering Tony's going to be mentally undressing me, but I put on black trousers and a sparkly sheer black top. It looks a bit weird for a Tuesday morning as I set a small vase of violets in the centre of the virginal white tablecloth.

'What the hell are you at?' shouts Mum when she sees me. 'It's summer and you look like a black crow! All those buttons open, I can count your ribs. You look like an x-ray from the hospital!'

I'm just about to go up and change when the doorbell rings. Tony doesn't realise that in these rural parts the front door is only for strangers or the Minister and everyone else ploughs in through the back. I run to welcome him and there he is, slightly hippyish in his loose shirt, jeans and black cowboy boots, hair carefully disheveled, more a relaxed entrepreneur than a businessman. As he hugs me I smell the musk off him.

He says something in his deep voice and I don't even hear it. All I'm aware of is the sound of it, the tone of something familiar from the past like a far-off church bell or the rasp of leaves or the sonorous slap of the waves. It's one of those deliciously rare occasions when I'm in the moment, yet observing from afar.

On his way in, he checks himself out in the hall mirror and pauses a few moments to pluck at his hair like an expert flower arranger. Mum and Dad are already coming out of the kitchen to greet him.

'Oh god, you caught me fixing my hair,' he laughs, embarrassed.

'That's grand, I always do the same myself as I pass,' says Mum graciously.

We go into the living room to chat.

'That's a great car you have,' says Dad.

'It's just a hire car,' says Tony airily, 'but I love to drive whenever I'm out of Warsaw. I have a driver there.'

'I've my own driver too,' jokes Mum, grinning at Dad.

'I'd go on a road trip if I could trust my staff. I've worked it out that if my employees are fifteen minutes late, I lose two hours work a week which is two full weeks a year. So, whenever they're late, I ask "What's the euro to the dollar?"

As soon as they answer, I tell them "Good, and I expect the same accuracy with time."'

Dad nods approvingly, but somehow I can't help feeling relieved I didn't land a job in Tony's office.

As Mum and Dad leave us to make coffee, Mum mouths the words 'He's a nice guy' at me in encouragement.

Now Tony and I are alone I steer the chat round to why he's come.

'Because I missed you,' he says and he moves across the sofa towards me to play with my hair. 'I thought of you so much and realised I hadn't been to Ireland in years, so I decided to mix it with a bit of business.'

'I've missed you too.' I'm loving the light pull of his fingertips.

'How old are you again?'

'Thirty-two.'

'Well, you still have time,' he adjudges, 'but better not leave it too long if you want kids.'

I'm wondering if he's offering and the question is tremoring on my tongue when Mum barges in carrying a platter stacked with homemade traybakes. She's defrosted a whole month's worth of Ulster classics – peanut butter balls, fifteens, Rice Krispies buns, date slices, chocolate biscuit cakes, lurid choc-mint squares, raspberry ruffle bars, snowballs, fudge tartlets and, of course, millionaire's shortbread.

'Enough to choke a donkey,' Dad announces proudly. 'Fill your boots there, Tony.'

'Sorry, I don't eat cakes. Got to watch this,' he says, patting his belly which is just about verging on the portly.

'Oh, this one doesn't care at all,' says Mum, patting Dad's stomach.

'Here, don't touch what you can't afford,' laughs Dad, but it's clear my parents are put out by Tony's refusal. I can see them thinking, what sort of a crater has she brought to our home, even though they give him a bit of a bye ball for being English.

'I have to tell you, Tony,' says Dad, 'I'm glad Cara's left all that teaching behind. She was just putting by her time.'

'Oh, I said the same to her myself,' says Tony.

'All those years of university and earning peanuts in Poland.'

'She never did let her education go to her head,' says Mum with heavy irony.

At least they're all bonding over their deep disappointment in me. After Mum and Dad head back to the kitchen I test one of my articles on Tony, reading it out loud. It's a swingeing opinion piece about working abroad post-Brexit.

'So, what do you think?'

'It's funny,' he says, 'but you're not going politically far enough. You need to rip your subject to bits.'

A text beeps through and he checks it, holding the phone at a distance from his eyes.

'Kasia?'

'Yeah. She's just finished teaching her aerobics class. She recently took up kickboxing, but gave it up because she doesn't approve of violence outside the home.'

I laugh and remember that's why I like him – his sense of humour is so black you'd think he'd grown up in the Troubles.

I watch him relax on the sofa, his limbs loosening.

'It's been ages since I've been in someone's front room,' and there's a wistfulness in his voice. 'Your parents are great too.'

'What? You told me you hate families.'

'Only my own,' he says. 'My mother's will went to my three sisters and I didn't get a penny.'

'She must have thought you didn't need it.'

'It's not the money, it's the principle. It should have been divided equally.'

It's strange to hear a millionaire talking about equality where money's concerned. He once told me the only time his family contact him is by begging letter.

'Listen, I have a proposal,' he says.

And, finally, what I've been waiting for all along, and his blue eyes seem filled with a cross between hope and concern.

'I can see your parents are worried about you and would love you to have a regular man on the scene. So ... I'll be your regular and I can also help you with your articles and getting a career in journalism. I'll mentor you, set up with a blog. What do you say?'

I don't say anything and he burbles on about me inviting him over some weekend when my parents are on holiday.

'If not,' he says, 'I'll buy a house in Belfast and we'll do a residential weekend together.'

I tell him I'm not sure. He doesn't seem to realise my parents might be whipped up with matrimonial fever. Besides, I don't just want a temporary part-time zero hours contract Mr Meantime. Isn't it bad enough with the job market so precarious that relationships are the same?

'I know you're sore about not getting the job, Cara, but I didn't give it to you because I had a conscience and didn't feel it was right for you.'

I can feel myself weakening. In a business sense he could be good for me. He told me during my interview that I seemed confident but could be more so. And it's not only that making me melt; it's his scent.

'Think about it,' he says, standing up. 'Right. I better make tracks.'

'But aren't you staying for lunch?'

'I can't. I already changed my flight to an earlier time.'

We walk through to the kitchen. The gravy aromas circulate seductively.

My mother's face collapses like a soufflé when Tony tells her he's going.

'Oh no, could you not stay for at least a wee bite?'

'Sorry, but I have to get back. I'm off to Moscow, then BP this week.'

'BP?' My parents are bemused by his high-flying lingo.

'Budapest.'

Tony asks if he can have his lunch in a tupperware container and Mum looks affronted as if dealing with a customer who thinks he's pulled up at a McDonald's Drive Thru instead of her Michelin-starred restaurant, but politeness gets the better of her and she acquiesces, getting me to pull the roast out of the oven before its due time. It seeps blood as Mum carves into it.

Meanwhile, I walk Tony out to his car. The garden is full of butterflies flirting, sparrows tailing each other from hedge to hedge, and the soft purring coos from wood pigeons in the roseydandrum bush, as they call it in these parts.

He leans back against the passenger door and pulls me in to him for a kiss, and the press of his body and the weight of him feels warm, strong, familiar. His hand slides under my top, kneading my breasts, while my hand slips under his belt. Some neighbours are passing by, but they can't see anything as we're so close together.

'I want some time alone with you,' he whispers.

'So do I.'

I hear my mum's voice behind us and we decouple quickly.

'There you go,' she says, handing Tony two tupperwares. 'Safe home now.'

Dad's eyes jealously survey the hire car and we all wave goodbye to Tony as he spins out onto the main road past Murlough Bay.

'Well?'

Mum and Dad's hopes are in the air, as fragile as the faint ozone trembling across the shoreline. I don't answer.

'Do I need to be doing the lottery for the rest of my life?' asks Dad.

'I'm sorry,' I say. 'You heard him yourselves going on and on about money. That's all he ever does.'

'You stay bloody poor then,' retorts Mum. 'So what if he talks about it as long as you have it to spend?'

'You're as fucking thick as champ!' adds Dad furiously, half under his breath in case the neighbours hear. 'Can't see a good thing when it's offered to you.'

They stomp back indoors. Mum has a face like fizz on her, ranting away how I'll always be holding the devil by the tail. I go straight upstairs as I want to make the changes Tony suggested on my article while they're still in my head. When I think about his comments I should have figured them out myself. It's simply that I must go further in my comedy, I must be bolder. I don't need a mentor and especially not a man-tor like Tony.

Dad calls up that dinner is on the table. When I go down, my parents have both calmed down somewhat.

'He probably wasn't right for you anyway,' Mum concedes. 'Hiding his bald patch in our mirror.'

'Aye, just a beggar on horseback he is,' says Dad, pouring out the McGuigan's wine.

'Very inbetweeny. Not young enough to be a catch and not old enough to pop his clogs and leave you all his cash.'

'Sure aren't we dining like millionaires ourselves and isn't he off with just tupperware?'

'True,' smiles Mum.

'Exactly,' I say. 'It's like everyone says: it's better to be time rich than money rich.'

Mum and Dad exchange a look and I realise I spoke too soon.

'No, it's not,' says Dad coldly.

A bead of blood runs down the roast. The atmosphere is brittle with unsaid words. Our knives and forks scrape through the silence. From where I'm seated I can see the soufflés sitting in their ramekins slowly deflating.

HERE COMES THE DAY

The first day in the coffin was a doddle for Winston Ross. Well, a doddle was pushing it, but he'd once done five years in the slammer for importing cocaine from Amsterdam, hidden in the tyres of his Merc. Oh, he knew what it was like to be locked up, and sure the coronavirus lockdown had been a walk in the park compared to jail. His wife Andrea told him he needed his head looking at for staging something as extreme as his own burial, but his boss at the anti-drugs agency had already warned him to fundraise or his job would go.

What was the term his boss had used? Ah, yes, it was 'business critical' to find the necessary funds and, besides, what other job could Winston do now he'd turned fifty? Ethically he couldn't just walk away either. The whole virus outbreak had sent even more young people into the clutches of drugs, spiraling into suicide.

He was only doing the Christian thing – three days and three nights buried like Jesus Christ Our Lord. He'd originally asked Willowfield Church if they'd build a cave for him but the Rector Hayley Bell said it had a whiff of blasphemy about it and, moreover, from a logistical viewpoint it would cost a bomb to hire stones from the quarry, so they compromised on the coffin.

'Can we still do it at Easter?' asked Winston.

'No, I think Easter is about the resurrection and egg hunts, so let's leave Easter to the Lord, ok?'

'When should I do it then?'

'What about next month? For Lent,' suggested Hayley.

If this didn't grab teenagers' attention, nothing would.

It was the first day of March and Kerry Savage was heading back up the Woodstock Road from an all-nighter, dodging the puddles and the flocked mulch of old leaves and moss like she was playing hopscotch. She had a split in the sole of her left boot and the dampness was already blooming into the wool of her sock.

Up above, the sky was full of dozed, frayed cloud and seemed vaster than ever after twelve hours in a small party house kitchen. She'd popped half a bumble at four am just to inspire herself to chat up that man, and now as she walked she kept telling herself to relax her jaw – over the years she'd cracked three teeth after E. She was mad at herself for taking party drugs, but every so often she lapsed as they helped take the edge off her anxiety.

She passed the Glamazon Tanning Studio with its sexy cardboard woman in a red bikini in the window, and dreamed of the heat of summer. In the upper window there was a sign advertising Pole Kittens with a number to phone. She chuckled to herself, imagining the middle-aged moggies it would attract, inelegantly sliding down poles.

As she crossed the street, the mountains in the distance were as grey as the roof slates and a cold blast cut through her light coat. A wind that would blow a gipsy off his sister, she muttered to herself, shivering. She could hear the rush of the Loop River from under the grate.

She thought of that fella at the party. He'd had slightly downcast eyes, a bit like the Virgin Mary in paintings, and when she'd shaken his hand it had felt limp, like it didn't belong to someone who knew how to grab life or grab hold of a woman, but something deep in her soul was composing an ode to his warm memory. Besides, it was true she was in her late thirties now and needed to compromise.

It was when she reached the corner of Willowfield Parish Church and My Lady's Road that she did a double take. A digger was opening a hole in the ground while two guys in hi-vis vests and hard hats were taking a coffin out of a van. She walked on puzzled. She prided herself on knowing everything about these streets, every burglary, every shoplifting, every pipe bomb through a letter box, and once she wondered about something she couldn't get it out of her head. It was a condition of her condition. So she went back.

'Are you burying someone?' she asked one of the workmen.

'We are indeed,' laughed the guy, raising his voice as the digger gouged out the wet, claggy earth. 'Winkie Ross is going underground in an hour for charity.'

'Winkie Ross?'

'Aye, he's highlighting what happens to you when you do too many drugs.'

'You can donate online to help the addicted,' chipped in the other guy.

'I'd rather not,' said Kerry, turning.

As she walked away she felt fury bubble up in her heart, a heat spreading through her that the cold wind couldn't temper. She started to walk faster, hardly noticing a friendly hello aimed at her in passing. She turned into a terraced street, angrily lashing out at an artificial topiary ball hanging outside a care home.

Winston turned three hundred and sixty degrees, knowing it would be his last look at the world for three days. A meniscus of brighter cloud curved around the Castlereagh Hills and he took it as god's promise. He felt a little faint as he purposely hadn't eaten in twelve hours to ensure his bowels were clear. All he'd had were a few sips of water.

The coffin was lodged deep in the earth. It had taken some trouble to procure.

'How much is your cheapest coffin?' Winston had asked a few weeks ago.

'Firstly, may I ask who it's for?' replied the funeral director.

'It's for me and I need it by the first of March. Would that be ok?'

'Oh, I'm very sorry to hear that. Will you be requiring a full funeral package?'

Winkie laughed. 'Not at all, I'm not even near death's door. Here, you're probably thinking I'm a vampire.'

'Well, you wouldn't be the first one,' the funeral director replied drily.

The prices were steep, so Winston phoned a guy he knew who made the wooden hoops for Lambeg drums.

'Aye, I'll whack one up no bother,' the man said. 'I'll order some pine in today and make it so nice and roomy you'll think you're in your living room.'

A living room it certainly wasn't but it was a good enough size even so. An imitation headstone was sitting next to it that said:

Winston Ross
www.druglines.org
#graveproblem

'Do you like it?' asked Hayley Bell.

'I never thought I'd be asked if I like my own headstone, but yeah, I love it.'

He was pleased to see a couple of teenagers from Robert's youth group. They were standing with their heads poked forward out of their hoodies like shy turtles peering out of their shells. He gave them a nod, and was even more delighted to see a BBC crew heading over to him.

'Winston, is this just a publicity stunt?' the interviewer asked.

'No, but we all need a bit of theatre to remind us where we'll end up if we take drugs. Fifteen years ago I nearly died myself – I was in hospital on dialysis for weeks, so this message needs to get through.' He stared directly into the camera, as he'd seen Bob Geldof do at *Live Aid* years before. 'You do drugs, you die. So, fund us now.'

He took his coat off and handed it to Andrea.

'Are you sure you'll be warm enough, love?' she checked.

'Course I will. The earth's an extra blanket.'

He took his shoes off on the polythene plastic at the side of the coffin and gave Andrea a kiss. A couple of friends helped him down onto the mattress at the coffin's base. It seemed comfortable enough. There was just enough room for him to sit upright against a couple of pillows.

'Give us a grin, Winkie,' called a photographer from the *Belfast Telegraph*.

'Good luck, Winkie!' shouted his friend Robert.

Winkie did the thumbs up for the camera, feeling for a second like an astronaut strapped in for take off. The wooden lid closed over the top of his head. There was a pipe of about six inches in diameter affixed to the top of the lid and he could see a circle of sky, and then a round segment of shadowy face with an eye and half a nose looking down at him.

'Alright in there, Winston?' bellowed Andrea.

'Grand!'

A porthole to heaven, he thought to himself, looking up. All he needed to focus on was the huge cheers he'd get when he resurfaced in three days' time.

He could hear the screech of a drill securing the lid. Then the slow gravelly rumble of soil like hail on a roof. And the drag of the headstone.

Not even Houdini could have got out of this one.

Kerry pulled out a bag from the freezer, prawns cascading onto the floor like clinking coins from a penny arcade. She was jittery anyway from the all-nighter but the reemergence of Winkie Ross had sent her into free fall. How could she not have known he lived in this part of the east too? He must have just moved here. For the sake of her mental health she hadn't thought about him in years.

What a hypocrite, she raged, him posing as one of the good guys, Mr God Squad, Mr Anti-Drugs, when he used to hoover them up like a Dyson V8. Didn't anyone know what he'd done?

She'd only been eighteen and him in his early thirties, thin, wiry and wired. He was a fixture at parties, selling coke and speed, then one day it was like an after party to the party. He'd lit up the teaspoon, tied her upper arm, spanked her vein like she'd done something bad. But her sister Stella was already high on coke. Winkie knew that and still he gave her skag. God, to think of it ... No, she couldn't go there for the howling grief.

At the time she'd been going out with Winkie's paranoid mate Brodie Shirlow. She couldn't help blaming Brodie for what had happened to Stella, since it had occurred in his flat, so she'd split up with him, breaking his heart in the process. Brodie called round a few weeks later with a couple of drinks 'to part on good terms' as he'd put it, but the bastard had spiked her drink with huge quantities of lysergic acid for dumping him.

She'd been in a coma for three weeks. When she'd come round, her brain was hyper and she was banging into the hospital walls, so they'd sent her to a psychiatric unit for a month while she gradually began to come back to herself. But she'd never be the same as before, the consultant neurologist told her. She couldn't concentrate on things, she had anxiety and ADHD, her eyelids fluttered when she focused too long on people's faces. And the only thing that comforted her was repetitive behaviour, walking through the same streets, taking the same route, eating exactly the same food.

She went to the police about Brodie Shirlow but he was never charged. He counterclaimed she'd taken the acid herself and, after all, she was a well-known druggie, ask anyone he'd said, and it was true that her doctor had the records to prove it.

The word on the street was that it had been Winkie who sold Brodie the acid. And now the creep had the brass neck to be profiteering from his old ways, setting himself up as some reformed exemplar in society, the dirty fucker.

She Googled him, noticing how fresh he looked for his age bearing in mind his sallow, blotched years, looking at him standing all smug next to the rector, the fucking rectum more like, and next to Andrea and how dumpy, middle-aged and respectable she appeared, pride of the parish no doubt. She thought about him in his coffin. She started having wild thoughts, like she'd stepped out of a Tarantino movie, of throwing a black mamba into it, watching him thrash around, then expire from its bite. But where could she get a snake from? She knew a couple of people with vivariums, or was it vivaria, but wouldn't it be cruel on the snake? Ha, the poor snake might get beaten to death by his bible!

She went out to her back yard. The rain was bucketing now, but she didn't care. She upturned a discarded slate to find a worm and a couple of darting woodlice underneath. She picked up the worm, its body contracting, wincing at her touch, and she thought of throwing it into his coffin to eat his rotting, corrupting corpse.

But it was hardly payback on a grand scale, it was hardly poetic justice for his crimes. She felt her left eyelid tremor as she carefully set the worm back under the slate. Be good to the innocent and bad to the guilty, she told herself. The rain was trickling down the tendrils of her fringe, making her realise how long she'd been standing there. It was all just part of her condition. A huge tiredness washed over her. She hadn't slept for ... wait, she had to count it up exactly ... twenty-seven hours.

She went back inside and turned off the oven. Vengeance is a dish served cold went through her mind. There was no rush as she had a full three days and three nights. She could even be the bigger person and let him go. But no, it was strange, it was almost like god had delivered him to her that morning. Not that she could implicate herself as she didn't want to jeopardise her new job teaching drama to prisoners at Hydebank, but ...

Shaky-fingered, she opened the jar of Librium and washed it down with water. Librium for the equilibrium, she told herself as she'd done thousands of times in her life. She went up to bed. At the landing window, a tiny white feather outside was quivering against the glass.

Winkie's phone kept beeping. Social media was going wild – sixty-eight likes so far for one tweet. He sat for an hour tapping away on the bright screen before the coldness began to sink in. The problem was the damp wind swirling down the pipe. It howled like his chimney pots at home. He needed to move to keep warm, so he started doing sit ups, but bounced up too vigorously, hitting his head against the wood. He lifted up the duvet instead and wriggled under it. He consoled himself with the thought that when the clouds parted that night he could look up at the stars as if through an astronomer's telescope.

A voice shouted down the pipe and he recognised it as Hayley Bell's. 'I'm just going to put the lid on as it's starting to rain. Is that ok, Winkie?'

The lid scraped across the pipe. It was a loose sloping cover but there was still a gap of air to be had, and if it got too stifling he could punch it open himself. Hayley had chosen to cover the first shift, no doubt to enjoy the photo op and glad-handing that went with it. Half the church was rostered over the next few days to sit by him for two hours each, and at night two people at a time were scheduled to keep vigil. He couldn't be left alone for how could you trust the wee skiprats and drug dealers round here not to cover his pipe.

It was nearly pitch black and he wondered if panic would get a hold of him. He searched down the side of the mattress for his torch and switched it on. He immediately felt better; the coffin was plenty spacious and it was really no worse than lying in the bottom of two bunk beds. Already he felt warmer. Let's face it, he'd ended up in worse kips back in the day, in crack dens and under bridges. And it was nothing compared to five years of incarceration. In jail he used to do drawings of his cell window with its heavy metal bars, then rub the bars out with his left hand, imagining the freedom. Down here the big thing he objected to was the smell of rotting vegetation which seemed to seep through the wood, but he imagined he'd get used to it and wasn't it a small penance for continuing to do the job he loved.

His phone buzzed again. More donations on his crowdfunder. Six thousand quid already, get in there! At this rate his job would be secure for another year. When he thought about it he was proud of his turnaround in life. He rarely dwelled on his old self – 'his old self' sounded like a contradiction when it was really his younger self – and he chose to accept the old rock 'n' roll myth that he'd blitzed a whole decade of his memory away, but it was true that very few had survived. Even Brodie Shirlow had committed suicide. Those had been Winston's days BC – Before Christ – and now he was living AD – After Drugs. It was wonderful how the church gave you that chance to be reborn, and on the rare occasion he managed to persuade a young person to repudiate the drugs, it was redemption for each one he'd known who had died.

These three days, he assured himself, would be a retreat and even the fasting would be easy as there was no food to tempt him. He was buried on consecrated ground, remember, where no danger, spiritual or physical, could touch him. It was good to be in a quiet, peaceful place and it was almost akin to being a hermit walled in by members of his own order.

He checked his phone again. Six thousand seven hundred and thirty pounds. Come on, god, you can go higher, he urged, his spirits soaring. He tapped in his thanks to the donors, then switched off his phone as he didn't want to run out of juice.

The patter of rain on the lid was easing and suddenly it opened. Another circular segment of face peered in at him.

'Alright, Winston?' his boss shouted.

'Time I got a pay rise!' Winston shouted back.

His boss laughed.

Kerry turned into My Lady's Road, her footsteps quickening in beat with her heart. The freezing pavement made the soles of her shoes sound like they had steel inserts. The wind had calmed, turning the walled streets into an echo chamber.

The footlights around Willowfield Church illuminated two people sitting on chairs. It was 4.10am and she'd timed it to arrive right in the middle of 'the graveyard shift' she told herself, alive to the irony.

That afternoon she'd woken from a deep sleep, the vestiges of last night's alcohol singing in her system, and it was then that the idea of what to do about Winkie came to her with such clarity it seemed almost communicated through a dream.

The two seated men peered over at her.

'Sorry I'm late,' Kerry called out. 'Hayley told me I was on from four.'

'Oh, right,' said the older man of the two. 'There must be a bit of a mix up cause we're on from four till six too.'

'Oh dear. But she definitely said four o'clock to me.'

'Well, look, I'll nip on home then if you don't mind doing it,' said the older guy, giving her his chair. 'Sure it's baltic out here and I'm only over the cold.'

'Great,' she said, jumping into his seat. 'Cheers and goodnight now.'

The remaining man extended his gloved hand. 'I'm Robert by the way.'

'Amanda. Is Winston asleep?'

'Looks like. Not a peep out of him so far.'

She nodded. It was all going so well she was sure the kicker would come at any second. She could feel his eyes scrutinising her.

'Funny ... I've never seen you in church,' he said.

'Oh, I don't go here, but I've known Hayley for years. An old friend of the family.'

'Right,' he nodded. 'Do you know Winkie then? I mean Winston?'

'Oh, vaguely. Met him years ago in passing at a party. Seemed a sound enough guy.'

'Right. Back in his wild days?' smiled Robert, fishing a little, and she guessed he wanted to hear the dirt on him.

'Yeah, the noughties were mental, you know?'

'Were they? The maddest I got was headbanging to Christian rock I'm afraid,' he laughed.

He was so easy to talk to. She noticed he didn't have downcast Modigliani eyes like the man at the party.

'What about your wife then?' she asked, fishing herself. 'Was she wild?'

'I don't have a wife, Amanda. Well, I did but she died of cancer.'

'Oh, I'm sorry to hear that.'

A vision passed through her head of chatting to Robert all night, of giving him her phone number, of seeing him again. It was time to move on and she had to admit to herself that maybe Winkie, much as she hated him, had a point, reinventing himself, changing his values.

Robert shifted his chair closer to hers, his eyes darkening, the shadows surrounding them almost satanic, but his breath was white in the cold and there was a lightness, a goodness shining out of his words. He was telling her how Winkie had helped him set up his youth group. His evident admiration for such a murderer stunned her, pulling her back to her senses and her old rage.

'I'm bringing my youth group here to show them the truth of drugs,' he said, but she was already pretending to search her pockets.

'Aw no,' she burst out. 'I think I dropped my keys on the way here. I thought I heard something hit the ground on London Road.'

'I have a torch. Do you want me to have a quick check?'

'Would you? I don't really want to be roaming the streets by myself.'

'Of course not. Look, it'll only take me five minutes if you hold the fort here.'

'Thanks. I really appreciate it.'

'No probs. London Road, right ...?' His words trailed off as he hurried away.

She knew it would take him at least ten minutes. Even so, she had to be quick in case someone else showed up. She took the rolled joint out of her pocket and lit it. After a huge inhale, she stepped over to the pipe, hunkered down, put her face into the circle and slowly blew out.

Winston spluttered in his dream. Hayley Bell was standing in the pulpit of Willowfield Church, one hand on the bible, the other holding a big fat joint of grass – but how was that possible? The shock of it jolted him awake. Oh my god, the smell of ganja was all around him. It was real. What the fuck?

A quiet voice spoke from above. 'Do you remember the day you sparked up Stella's vein with the skag? You'd already seen her do coke, she was flying, and you still went ahead and killed her. You ran out on us cause you were scared, remember? You pathetic little coward.'

The sound of slow sulphurous hatred chilled him. His mind scanned through a series of images. Stella, Stella, no idea, but it must have been that young girl who died in Brodie Shirlow's gaff. He couldn't even picture her.

'Look, sorry, I was out of my head. I didn't even know the girl. I didn't know what I was doing back then.'

'Not good enough, Winkie.'

Who the fuck was this woman? Where were the others? What had she done to them? A flapping was in his chest like batwings. He scrabbled for his phone but already he knew it was too late to call for help.

An object knocked against the pipe and some liquid hit his chest, followed by the fumes of it. It was petrol.

'Oh Jesus, no!'

He could hardly breathe with it. He began to choke and retch. Oh god, he was about to asphyxiate. He pressed his mouth to the pipe trying to suck in the air above.

'Please!' he wheezed. 'Don't kill me! I didn't mean to hurt her, I meant to give her a good time. I'm so sorry, believe me ...'

He heard the click of a Zippo and his insides turned to liquid.

Kerry stuffed the empty petrol canister into her bag and walked away quickly from the coffin, the pleading hysterical rasps of Winkie Ross fading behind her. Robert could be back at any minute and she had to get away. To think she'd actually held Winkie's life in her hands. As she turned onto the Woodstock Road she felt exhilarated. She had confronted him, given him a glimpse of the horror and guilt she'd gone through when her sister had died, and he would have to live with that now. She kept walking, fired up with such a heat in her chest she opened her coat. It struck her that no drug before had ever given her such a high.

She finally stopped and looked around. She'd trekked all the way to Knockbreda without even noticing. An hour must have passed as the sky was lightening overhead and cars were beginning to stream onto the dual carriageway. For the first time in years she hadn't even registered the roads. She could see Knockbracken Hospital surrounded by fir trees, where she'd spent a lonely month recovering from the acid, but she turned away from it, heading into the

Castlereagh Hills, knowing where she wanted to go, who she wanted to talk to.

She kept on striding up a steep narrow country road. The sweat was springing from every pore. She felt like divesting her coat, chucking it over a hedge. Above the crest of the hill the sky was full of bright orange bars of cloud, like filaments burning. The new day was dismissing the neon party lights of the night, blasting them away with its bright power. It drew her on through her tiredness.

She rounded one last corner and she was there. The gates of Roselawn Cemetery, where Stella lay, were wide open. She remembered the pine coffin on the day of the funeral, the simplicity of the spring flowers laid on top, the collective shock on the mourners' faces at her sister's early death. It had taken a long time to return.

'Hello, Stella,' she whispered, stopping a while to rest on a mound of grass.

She looked back at the sunlit city where the living were rising once more to go about their daily business.

THE LOVE VIRUS

I was fifty and said to myself I wasn't going to let my life ebb away without making things happen. I'd been in love once with a handsome Greek guy and enthralled by, or at least in thrall to, a few other men, but there had only been one man I'd truly loved and the relationship had ended in my early twenties. It seemed I'd peaked at love young and it was typical of me being an early starter. According to Mum I'd started walking at nine months like I wanted to grab the world by the throat. It's funny to think I ended up sitting on my bum as a writer. Anyway, much of my forties I spent ill with a spinal condition and missed out on men. For those five years I was so intent on survival I couldn't think about anyone's body but my own.

On New Year's Eve, freshly turned fifty, I sat drinking with friends and wrote down my aspirations for the year – travel and sex. Prior to that they'd been health and prosperity, but I was throwing them out the window to make way for hedonism. What I yearned for was a decade of decadence. For what other reason had I garnered years of wisdom than to decide that the ultimate wisdom was to submit to folly? Two days after New Year's Eve I had sex with a nice man with misshapen toes and, a month later, I flew to Brussels with a play of mine, so it was a great start to the decade.

Then coronavirus came. Then lockdown came. Then my playwriting career went.

It was odd because the downturn in my career had been predicted by a numerologist six months before on a trip to Australia. I'd met the numerologist at a theatre festival; he was an aspiring writer like every human being who could wield a pen. I didn't want to let him do my numbers because I don't like being at the mercy of charlatans, but the actress in my play persuaded me and, besides, I was born on the 7th and am lucky sevens all the way. I furnished the numerologist with a few numbers and he added them up out loud and divided them like he was Einstein working out an equation. He also had white hair like Einstein and a lugubrious voice. Although he seemed to need a couple of attempts he finally came up with a number for me.

'So?' I asked, hoping for great things, while also hoping he wasn't about to predict my untimely demise.

'Your writing is going to take a dip over the next two years.'

'Aw, what?'

'You'll be successful again later but prepare for a disappointing two years. Look, it's not me, it's the numbers.'

I felt like punching him and saying it's not me, it's my fists. My writing had been on the rise for some time and the only way I reckoned it would go downhill was if my health took a hit. The prospect was somewhat disconcerting. However I decided to take his prediction simply as the jealousy of a less successful writer and forgot all about it. That is until it came true.

Living on my own, lockdown was lonely but I consoled myself that it was infinitely better than being confined with an irritating partner I'd be tempted to murder. At least alone the only person you ever want to murder is yourself. Theatres were closed, but I went out for my daily walk that spring and witnessed the suspension of human life in the streets, and took some joy in the effervescence of wild flowers spilling onto the pavements. The sun was out every day as if loving how nature had reclaimed the world from our predation.

Let's just say I am a person who neither enjoys rules nor respects them, so after a few weeks of isolation I was already looking for an escape route. I was suffused with this awkward energy. I felt like a mayfly that had woken up in winter and was flying around in the wrong season. Back in February I'd been flirting with a stage manager-slash-DJ, and by April I noticed him live-streaming his sets on Facebook under the moniker of #TheLockdownLover, so I took him at his word and DMed him to come round to mine for a drink. He got back and said he'd love to, but never fixed a date. He seemed more interested in working out how to travel to Ibiza with his rabbit called Jessica. I think #TheLockdownLover might have been better phrased as #TheLockdownLoser, but seriously if I christened myself thus I'd make sure I lived up to it. Perhaps I'd misunderstood and he was simply a lover of lockdowns.

During these months I WhatsApped my friend Seán. Seán makes a decent living out of writing stories in the Irish language and, believe me, if I spoke Irish or even Ulster Scots, I'd be ripping the arse out of it too. Things were going so badly writing wise I suggested changing my name.

'Why not?' Seán said. 'Do that initial thing like J.K. Rowling and then you'll pass for a man.'

Initials? That would make me K.J. Kelly and, unfortunately, all I could think of was KY Jelly!

Anyway I wasn't about to do anything drastic. I just had to ride this rough year out and submit to my fate. Everyone kept posting motivating memes on Facebook like 'Your current situation is not your final destination' or 'Depression rearranged is I pressed on'. However, depression is also an anagram of 'pedo sirens' which isn't quite so jolly. Everyone was also showing off their newfound skills like breadmaking or woodturning, but the only accomplishment I'd acquired was emptying a wine bottle at record speed. The cloistral surrounds of my tiny Belfast house weren't exactly uplifting but, as the weeks passed, lockdown restrictions began to lift a little so I phoned my landlord about the leaking roof on my boiler house. A few days later a builder arrived.

'Hello, Kate, I'm Davey. Your landlord was on the phone.'

He spoke to me with so much cheery familiarity I almost thought I recognised him. I explained the problem and he followed me out to the yard. He tapped on the black plastic sheeting above the boiler house door.

'Keeping the boiler cosy, are you?'

'No,' I smiled. 'It's to keep the pigeons out. They keep having sex on my back wall, then flying in here to build their nest.'

His eyes flared in amusement at the notion of the rampant sex life of pigeons. 'Well, we can't have that. I've got some plastic spikes to deter them.' He jumped up onto the boiler tank to have a good look at the roof, then leapt back down. I liked him. He had sparkly blue eyes and a cheeky grin that exposed his teeth which were perfect except for a false front one where the gum was dark-edged. I love imperfections.

Soon the sun was hijacked by June rain clouds and the days became so humid my silver jewellery kept turning black and my red hair turned the shade of iron oxide. The damp was seeping everywhere, turning the coffee granules black and sticky and crumbling the washing tablets. It wasn't the weather for traversing roofs so there was no sign of Davey. I spent my days writing and walking, enjoying the sights of lockdown. It was a visual world shorn of the usual auditory chatter. The city was shuttered as if every morning a funeral cortege was passing by, but there was a sensuous softness later in the day that drew people into the streets with their chairs and bottles of wine like they were sitting in low-end trattorias. In the evenings the moon was a white beach ball washed up in the white waves of clouds ready to play.

There is something about the run up to midsummer with the days lengthening into short pale nights; I've always derived a huge energy from them. In bed I tossed and turned and coughed under my damp duvet, hardly sleeping after the long hours of lockdown inertia. I couldn't get over the cancellation of my trip to Bulgaria and I kept running this parallel life in my head, visualising myself travelling with the piquancy of what could have been. I wanted to go wild, drug myself to the stars, go white water rafting, jump off a cliff into the iridescent blue sea, but actually, apart from the drugs, I'd never done any of these. I've always believed you don't have to go bungee jumping to know you're alive – all you do is press your neck and feel the quick throb of your own pulse.

When the sun returned so did Davey with his sunny demeanour. He parked in the entry and I opened the yard door. 'Right,' he said. 'I'll get tore in here.'

From the kitchen window I watched him put in a new beam. I couldn't keep my eyes off him because I'd been starved of human company for the past two and a half months. He kept muttering encouragement to himself and would sometimes break out into whistling short refrains. With his puffed-out chest he looked and sounded like a demented parrot and almost flew up the ladder onto the roof. He had solid shoulders, a builder's tan on his arms and lines scored in his brown forehead like a woodcut. When he came back down the steps I went out to him.

'Right, now to sort out the walters,' he said with a broad smile.

'The walters?'

'The pigeons. Walter Pidgeon.'

'Oh yeah. I'm just slow.'

'Now for a Danny La Rue,' he said, getting out a screw.

'For the two-by-four,' I added, as he drilled into the door.

He liked that I knew rhyming slang. Belfasters have more rhymes than cockneys. He dropped to his knees to drill in another set of bird spikes.

'Have you got iron kneecaps?' I asked.

'Know what my secret is? Every month I wrap my knees up in bandages soaked in *poitín*. Do you mind if I smoke?'

'Not at all. You're in the open air.'

He took out a fag and lit it. 'It's my big vice. Have you no vices?'

Sex flew through my head but I quelled it. 'Yeah, I love drinking. Can't wait for the pubs to open again.'

'Ah, I don't drink.'

'No wonder. You can't be clambering about on roofs with a hangover.'

'I know. I've lost friends before. One only fell four feet but he hit his head and – stone dead.'

'God.'

'Life's dangerous.' He showed me his thumb. It was skew-wiff, curved to one side at the knuckle like it was facing the wrong way. He told me how it was bitten off by a dog, and then segued into another story about witnessing a bomb when he was a paperboy. 'Sorry,' he said, pausing. 'If you haven't noticed, I talk too much.'

'It's great. I haven't heard anyone for months – except on Zoom.'

'Right,' he said, stirring himself. 'Better get tore in again.'

'Would you like a cup of tea?'

'A Rosie Lee? I'd love one.'

He set his ladder against the wall to check the gutters while I got the kettle on. He was talking to himself again. He was like his own radio channel. Ten minutes later he came down with an empty can of Coke in his hand.

'Look what was stuck in the downpipe!' he shouted through the window.

I laughed all the more because I was thinking of the topless hunky builder in the 90s ads for Coca Cola, the ultimate female fantasy which Davey for all his charm did not quite live up to. I brought him out tea and a biscuit, but he declined the latter.

'Got to watch this,' he said, patting his waist. He had a stomach but it didn't sag like those of the lazy. This might sound strange, but it was pert like a young pregnant woman's and I found it attractive.

I handed him a cup with my photo on it. My friends had bought it for my birthday as a joke with the words 'Be careful what you say or you may end up in my play'.

'What sort of a play?' asked Davey and I could see from his mischievous eyes that he was wondering if I wrote about sex.

I was suddenly aware that in these narrow back yards my neighbours could hear everything, so I answered 'A comedy, of course.'

'Oh, a comedy,' he echoed with a touch of disappointment before looking at my photo again and saying 'Still. Wow.'

'Ah, you're very kind.'

'No, I was talking about the tea. Ha, got you there!'

'Ha!' I liked his cheekiness. 'I'm probably keeping you back from your work.'

He eyed the darkening skies. 'No. I might take the afternoon off as I've another roof job and the rain's coming. But I suppose I should be on my way.'

'Yeah.' I noticed he wasn't making a move. I took in his teak skin and his silver hair and wanted him so badly, but in seconds he'd be gone.

'I'll have to love you and leave you,' he said and there was a wistful look in his eyes.

'Love you,' I repeated, knowing I had to say something. 'What about some love?'

He looked surprised that I'd blurted it out. 'Yes, love if you want it.'

'Yeah, I really want it.'

Before I knew it I was kissing him in the kitchen. As he followed me to my bedroom he checked 'Is it alright if I come up with my boots on?'

'No worries.'

'My work trousers are dirty.' They were spattered in paint but it didn't matter; nothing mattered.

'Sure look at the state of my room,' I said, pointing out the piles of paper.

He sat down on the bed and unlaced his big fibreglass boots. His socks had scorch marks on the toes.

'See?' he joked. 'Shows I work as fast as fire.'

As I took my bra off I remembered the cups were stuffed with tissue paper to make them look bigger. 'Sorry about this,' I said. Between his burnt socks and my tissued bra we were hardly the king and queen of porno fantasy. But we still looked pretty good and he was hard.

'How old are you?' I asked.

'Fifty-six.'

'Are you married?'

'No.'

He pushed me down onto the bed.

'I love these,' he said of my breasts.

'You're sweet.'

'Sweet as, as they say on the street.'

I got out a condom from the bedside drawer and he asked me to put it on him. I put it on the wrong way round as I do eighty percent of the time. Even at aged fifty I was all fumble-fingered. The next problem was I was too dry. It seemed ironic that in this whole damp wet country, my vagina was the one exception.

'I'll make you wet,' he said, moving down me, licking along the centre of my body in one sensuous line. When he returned to kiss my mouth he crinkled his eyes and I could feel his lips widen on mine in a smile. Once he entered me, he was fast. He still kept talking, encouraging himself on.

'Some pup, eh?' he said of himself, framing it as a question before urging me. 'Come ... come, baby.'

I found it surprising that a guy in his fifties didn't know that firstly women don't come in time to men and secondly women rarely come during penetrative sex. I guessed he wasn't much of a reader. He was so excited he came quickly.

'That was amazing,' he said and I was feeling a beat in my heart that told me I was alive. 'And my name's Davey,' he added with a laugh, just to poke fun at how little we knew each other.

'And the best part is that it was illegal,' I exulted.

It was still against lockdown rules to invite people into your home but, of course, I doubted the police would come knocking at my door. Considering a raft of politicians had been caught for illicitly visiting their lovers I was in some pretty esteemed company.

'Do many women let you into their bedroom?' I asked.

'The last was a –' He cut himself off, not wanting to cast himself as too easy, and told a story from twenty years ago when a neighbour asked him over to fix her Hoover. The hilarious thing was that she'd deliberately removed the fuse.

As we lay in bed I spotted a tattoo on his upper arm. It was an old-fashioned amateurish affair of a huge red heart bearing the name Ellen. 'Who's Ellen?'

'Oh, my old childhood sweetheart,' he said, rubbing it. 'I should really get rid of it.'

He showed me the scar on his left pectoral from where his lung collapsed and mentioned that he was at severe risk from coronavirus, which begged the question why he was sleeping with a stranger, but, what the hell, it was his business. Not to be outdone in the danger trophies I showed him the scars from my back and told him I'd been confined to my bedroom for five years.

'Oh, I wish I'd known you then,' he quipped.

As we got dressed, he said he was often working nearby and wondered if he could pop in again.

'No,' I said. This was the awkward part. The last thing I wanted was a guy to call round for sex whenever he felt like it. I'd been in those fuck buddy relationships before and they either just fizzled out or, even worse, feelings became involved. As far as I was concerned the most ideal relationship was a holiday romance. A week of never-ending passion, ended by a handy flight home. The second most ideal relationship was a brisk and beautiful one night stand. These were a million times easier before the invention of social media, which is basically an intrusive tracking device. The problem was that Davey had my number.

When we went down to the yard the pigeons were back on my wall checking out the bird spikes. They didn't look remotely intimidated by Davey's deterrents.

'Your neighbours will be wondering what I've been up to, parked in the entry,' he said. He seemed troubled, however, that I hadn't agreed to see him again. 'The thing is I won't be able to stop thinking about you now. Can I not see you tomorrow?'

'No.' I would have said more but intuited he didn't want any reasons or excuses.

'Take care,' he said, 'but if you want I'll take you for a drive some time. Text or phone any time, I'm always about.'

'Ok,' I said, but I wouldn't.

For hours I could taste his burnt cigarette kisses. I took a shower but afterwards I could still smell his hormones on my skin, or perhaps they were mine reawakened. It was strange but I remembered my mum once telling me that she knew the builder working on her house longed for her by the way he hung around. She would never have cheated on my dad but the builder's admiration had thrilled her. That night I noticed fluff from his builders' socks on my sheet.

The next morning was Saturday and I couldn't stop thinking about him. It was like an afterquake in my body and half of me wished I hadn't been so harsh. I had to learn to be more open. At eleven there was a call from Davey.

'Did you get my text yesterday?' he asked.

'No.'

'Oh no! I must have sent it to your landlord by mistake. I said thanks for your love potion and could we do it with a bottle of wine next time with three kisses.'

Oh god. The last thing I needed was for my landlord to think I was running a sex shop, but I wondered if Davey's story was just a ruse in order to contact me.

'I'm just up the road from you,' he said.

'Well, come on round then.'

'Front or back?'

'Front is fine.' I couldn't wait to see him.

In five minutes he was at the door. 'I've come about that job,' he said loudly for the benefit of my neighbours.

Once the door was closed he kissed me then followed me straight up to the bedroom.

'I want to undress you,' he said.

'I'll undress myself. It's logistically easier.'

I made sure I closed the windows as my neighbours were off work and I didn't want them to hear our moans, sighs, howls, yips and whatever strange manner of sounds we were about to make, not forgetting the laughter. Unfortunately it meant with the sun beating in it was going to be like a furnace, but if this heat didn't remind me of a summer holiday romance nothing would. He'd just come from working on the house of a millionaire who was so stingy he'd skimped on the scaffolding.

'No pockets in a shroud,' he said. 'That fella wouldn't give you the sleeves off his waistcoat. Sure, he's that miserable if he was a ghost he wouldn't scare you.'

We both laughed.

'Do you always work on a Saturday?' I asked.

'Since my brother died I work all the time. I do nothing but work to forget about him.'

I knew exactly what he meant. Since my parents died of cancer I did nothing but write.

When he touched me I couldn't help noticing the filth of his hands and nails – it was like sleeping with a coalminer! No doubt they weren't much worse than yesterday but back then I was caught up in the excitement and didn't care. Now, though, I could see the black creases in his calloused fingers and they felt as dry and scratchy as his stubble. I could also taste last night's wine on his breath despite yesterday's claims of not drinking. There was something else I noticed. His wedding ring. I hadn't seen it before because of his tarnished hands.

'You're married!'

'Oh, this? It's just an old one,' he quipped lightly. 'I'll tell you the truth after.'

He was slower and calmer today, as yesterday had slaked his desperation. He worked down my body, giving me big open-mouthed suction cups of kisses. He moved positions so he was behind me but it didn't work as I was too tall for him. At one point he put his hands on either side of my head and rubbed his thumbs across my cheeks, catching the corner of my eye, and immediately I pulled his hands away because I was scared of contracting an eye infection. What was charming yesterday was gross today, but dirt is the corollary of dirty sex with a workman; it's a side effect of the fantasy so I subdued my reservations and tried to enjoy the ride.

'Oh darling,' he sighed. 'I love you.'

It alarmed me to hear this as if he was overly smitten and might never let me go. He didn't even know me. I knew my hairdresser better than I did this man, but I told myself to relax.

'I love you,' he said again.

'I love you too,' I heard myself whispering shyly into his ear and it was so weird in my mouth, almost beautiful to say. I hadn't said it to any man since my dad who died three years ago. And before that, maybe fifteen years since I said it to a boyfriend.

He couldn't come and the weight of him as he kept pushing down on my hips was beginning to ache. He had that distant look in his eyes as he tried to climax, almost suffusing me with the power of his private imaginings. But just on the brink, he failed.

'I'm getting sore,' I warned him. 'I think it's the condom. Rubber burns. Rabbie Burns!'

He laughed at my joke, but he was still 'going for the burn' like an athlete, my ankles bouncing off his calves. He didn't get there, but it didn't matter. I've always felt that climax is an anticlimax, but he tried valiantly, drilling his hand over his cock, vibrating it so it was quivering like a hummingbird. As we lay beside each other he explained he didn't have sex with his wife anymore and slept on the sofa.

'I should probably get divorced. After forty years together, it's over.'

'Is it Ellen?'

'Eileen,' he said, rubbing his tattoo.

I didn't believe one iota that he slept on the sofa. Guys often felt they had to lie. Ok, so I hadn't seen his ring at first but even if I had I didn't care. The reason I'd asked if he was married was out of curiosity.

'You are my blue-eyed girl. Y'know, just like Van Morrison's brown-eyed girl,' he added to make sure I got the allusion. It struck me he was already making me his. 'Better get going,' he said, throwing his legs over the side of my bed. I found it cute how his flaccid penis was sitting on top of his bulbous balls like a stuffed vine leaf or the stub of a wet-tipped cigar. I made him tea afterwards and gave him my cup.

'Ah, your special love potion,' he said fondly, drinking it down.

We could see through the kitchen window the pigeons flying into the boiler house. 'Jesus Christ, they're back again building their love nest!'

He went out to reattach my black plastic sheet over the useless bird spikes. Those pigeons were indefatigable.

'Just put up a sign saying no sex here,' I told him and he laughed.

While he worked he told me stories about how a friend of his had been cut to bits by a propeller in a boat accident and how he'd nearly killed another motorist when his ladders had slid off the top of his van. He was like a one-man disaster movie but it was a subliminal reminder to me to seize the moment.

'So, can I see you again?' he asked.

'No.'

'Not even to chat?'

'No. I don't want any sort of relationship.'

'Ah, you're obviously holding out for a rich husband,' he said, noticing the skeptical look on my face before hastily adding 'or else you're going to write that bestselling play.'

I walked him to the front door. The white clouds resembled exploding bombs in the darkening sky. The rain was already starting to fall in dark blotches on the dusty pavements.

'I hope this rain keeps up,' said Davey looking out.

'Why?'

'Cause if it keeps up, as in up in the sky, it won't come down,' he joked.

I watched him walk away noticing how the pockets in his work trousers made his legs look muscled. 'Best of luck,' I said with finality.

'I'll see you soon,' he said with a cheeky grin getting into his van.

I went back indoors. I felt sore and tender inside. I switched on the shower and got undressed. There was a cut at the base of my nipple where he bit or frottaged too hard. In my twenties I never got sex wounds like this. Obviously I needed a bit more training to get back into the swing of it. I was so glad I'd seized the moment. But the problem with seizing the moment was that I feared the repercussions. 'See you soon' came floating back into my mind. Hadn't he listened to a word I'd said? And let's face it, if he really wanted to see me again he could take my front door off in a few turns of a screwdriver.

The shower calmed me. I knew in recent years I'd stopped taking risks but it was time to change and be fearless again. 'I love you' kept replaying in my mind. It struck me that I was too focused on trying to come up with cool soundbites for my life like 'I never see a play or a man twice'. I wrapped myself in a towel and went back up to my room.

I realised that it was 21 June, the longest day of the year, and it was still early and I had to make the most of it. Numbers mattered. There were bits of moss on the floorboards and I could see the imprint of his boots. I cleaned them away with my towel and got dressed.

KHAKI BEACH

For the third night in a row, the soldier he saw in Izium with his face blown off haunts his dreams.

'Keep your guard up,' the soldier appears to be warning him through the bandages.

'Get your arses up!' Rambo is shouting in through the bedroom door. 'The front line's waiting.'

Matt hauls himself into consciousness and rolls over onto his back, stretching his muscles after the rigour of a bad night's sleep.

Next to him, Mirren springs up like a dog to a master's voice. 'On our way!' she yells.

There's no median with her, thinks Matt. She's either larger than life or completely comatose and out for the count. He pulls on his shorts and hoodie and walks into the hall where Rambo is zipping up his camouflage jacket over his black vest top and affixing the Velcro patch of his battalion's wolf onto his sleeve. The apartment's still foggy from the joints he's smoked through the night.

'See you on the other side,' says Rambo, slinging his heavy backpack over his shoulder and shaking Matt's hand.

'Good luck to you.'

Rambo turns to Mirren, embracing her with his unencumbered arm. 'And take care, Braveheart.' He opens the door and limps out, the legacy of a fractured foot on the front line that hasn't fully healed.

Mirren impulsively follows him. 'Wait. I'll come and wave you off.'

Matt guesses they're going to kiss but the prospect doesn't bother him. It's been a week since he and Mirren moved into this shared apartment and it's already clear she'd be far better suited to Rambo. While Matt still shares a bed with her there's been no sex in the past five days. All he can think of is Yulia, the woman from the aid hub. He downs a glass of water then holds his hands out, splaying the fingers. Still shaking. They haven't stopped since the last trip to the east. His heart keeps quivering like a bombed-out bunker and he doesn't know if it's shell shock or the adrenaline of going on another tour so soon after the last.

At 6am he's in the driver's seat next to Mirren. The sun is angling on the wilted chestnut trees that line the road out of Kyiv. He keeps thinking of the chestnut leaf in faded aquamarine ink on Yulia's upper arm and the way her fingers gently pulled back her sleeve to reveal it. 'The symbol of Kyiv,' she'd told him. He passes a tank raised on a plinth and topped with a blue and yellow flag, glorifying the home forces. 'Ukrainian Resistance' it says in English on the hoardings and there are idyllic images of a handsome young Ukrainian soldier against a pure blue sky; a Slavic *shahid*, he muses to himself. The van is so weighed down with aid, it seems to drag on the dual carriageway. The suspension has recently been fixed and already it's straining.

Further out into the country a morning mist is floating over the sunflower fields, turning the distant forests the palest of blues. He enjoys how the dreamy whiteness is being burnt away by the sun. He pulls into a layby at the edge of the forest and they head down the path to the huts. The toilets are Turkish – stained holes in the ground reeking of piss – so they both nip into the undergrowth instead. Weeds tickle his calves, fill his nostrils with the scent of their own acidic excretions. A low sapling seems to flirt with his backside. Back in the van he takes an energy bar from one of the boxes. He's a couple of thousand *hryvnia* down from the last tour and flying through his savings, but he'll never be hungry with all the rations in the back.

Mirren decides to regale him with the story of how she and Rambo followed their drug dealer's instructions to pick up some MDMA in a Kyiv forest.

'So down I went arse-over-tip into a river and old pegleg Rambo had to rescue me. It was mental!' she laughs.

'Wish I'd seen you,' grins Matt.

'Me and Rambo were scrabbling around covered in mud together,' she says, glancing across at him from the steering wheel.

Trying to make him jealous, he thinks, and wonders why she bothers. They'd never even have got together if it hadn't been for the last tour. Surrounded by death and injury wasn't it obvious they'd cling to each other's life-filled bodies?

They pass yet another concrete hut topped by white sandbags, and soldiers wave them on. Now that the soldiers are outside Kyiv they carry their guns horizontally instead of aiming at the ground. An elderly woman is selling twig broomsticks at the roadside. A Soviet statue of a harvester in a headscarf stands tall at the head of the fields.

'I'm surprised the Ukrainians haven't blown her up,' says Mirren.

'She's too beautiful for that.'

He can feel Mirren looking at him sharply again. He thinks back to yesterday evening with Yulia, lying back in the park overlooking the witches' hill and stealing a kiss from her. Those blessed moments of quiescence. In the background a teenager was playing the Ukrainian national anthem on a grand piano. The classical music was so typical of Yulia, so cool and cultured compared to Mirren's youthful bacchanalian chaos. If only Yulia hadn't lived with her mum – or he hadn't shared a bed with Mirren – but it soothes him to know she's waiting for his return.

The checkpoints at the edge of the road are beginning to expand into earthen ditches and trenches, dust spiraling in the light breeze. Road signs are covered in camouflage nets, looking for all the world like abstract art paintings or a series of collages by some military Matisse. The towns are nameless now. A placeless country. In an anonymous country you can get lost.

'Look, a beach!' exclaims Mirren as they pass a lake lapping along a sandy shoreline. A sole fisherman is sitting at its edge.

'We're not stopping,' replies Matt firmly. 'We're on a mission.'

'Fuck sake, what a bore you are.'

'We'll stop on the way back. Ok?'

God, he rages to himself, she's such a melter, playing 'Echo Beach' on the stereo just to make her point. She's obsessed by beaches. Who does she think she is, Churchill? 'We shall fight them on the beaches ...' After the last tour, they'd been treated by their charity to a night in a swanky seaview hotel in Odesa. That evening Mirren had bounced over a wire fence onto the sand, only to have the manager of the hotel chase after her, imploring her to go no further because of the mines. She still waded into the sea in spite of him, or perhaps to spite him.

The lyrics induce a kind of nostalgic longing in him, although more for Kyiv than for anywhere else. He's thankful to be away from Chippenham and his job in an airplane factory. Day in day out assembling wings that flew other people to far-off countries while he remained in soporific situ. And he's even more glad to be away from the pain of not being able to see his two young kids. Every day he thanks god or some higher power that he's found a nomadic life of adventure.

They stop for lunch in a small town where the buildings are painted brightly over their cracked rendering. Sitting in the hot street reminds Matt of a past holiday in Spain, only a less idyllic version with swirling grit and petrol fumes. He doesn't recognise any of the Cyrillic script on the menu, so he asks for *holubtsi* in tomato sauce while Mirren goes for the potato pancakes. All washed down with a pint of Chernigivske. And a second. The best thing about the war is that no one cares if you drink drive. It's the lawlessness of Ukraine he loves. He notices how the waiter keeps staring at Mirren. She's different with her long dark red hair, vest top showing a glimpse of her pierced belly button, black combat trousers and Doc Martens. A sort of fantasy gaming avatar allied with restless charisma. Sometimes he thinks it's strange that she's a vegetarian whereas she doesn't so much as flinch at the sight of raw human meat.

A young guy walking by stoops to pick up a pigeon from the pavement. It tries to peck him but his thumbs and forefingers press tightly on its neck. He drops the pigeon down beside Matt and Mirren, letting it run in behind their table.

'Hello,' he smirks, barely breaking step.

'What the fuck was all that about?' asks Mirren, moving her chair to shoo out the pigeon.

'Not a clue.'

Back on the road they're waved to a stop beside a bank of cow parsley smelling of sweet aniseed. Soldiers are lazing on ripped-out car seating.

A soldier speaks to them first in Ukrainian before switching to English. 'Where are you going?'

'Kharkiv first, then Izium, Severodonetsk, Zaporizhzhia ...' Mirren shows him a permission letter from the Kharkiv chief of police. 'We have a van load of aid.'

'American?'

'I'm English, she's Scottish,' Matt says. It reminds him of the start of that old joke *An Englishman, an Irishman and a Scotsman walk into a bar ...*

Mirren opens the back of the van but the soldier gives it a cursory glance, trusting that everything's above board. As they pull away he's sneezing in the dust. It is as if he's saying 'Bless you, bless you,' anointing them with a nod of his head.

The forest firs are tilted, the foliage sparse and bark orange from the scorch of the sun. The trees appear to be marching towards the eastern front. He remembers the time he went with 'The Wall' gang to fight French football supporters in a forest outside Calais. The buzz he used to get from the violence. Christ, that big black French guy with arms big as branches, refusing to be felled. It wasn't until the following morning that the alcohol receded and he found out he'd fractured his arm from hitting the guy so hard.

'Oh holy Christ, Matt,' shrieks Mirren, seeing a fly buzz its circuitous dance across the windscreen. She rolls down her window and flaps her hand at it, swishing at her own hair as if it's landed there. 'Get rid of the fucking thing!'

The van chicanes wildly.

'Calm down!' says Matt, batting it out of the window. 'You're such a fucking pain. How come you can go to a war zone but one small fly and you lose it.' He hates it when she's a drama queen.

'Cheers, mate,' she says gratefully.

The road is eerily empty now. It's pocked with potholes and gravel and the white lines are barely visible. On the rare occasion Mirren drives past a van of journalists or aid workers she lifts her fingers off the steering wheel to acknowledge them. It's like being part of a rarified club. A convoy of army petrol tankers passes them by. Some cluster-bombed military vehicles are rolling in the opposite direction covered in sand and ash. Mirren cheers and raises her clenched fist out the window.

'*Slava Ukraini*, lads!' she shouts, but the soldiers barely react. Stupefied with exhaustion, thinks Matt.

They are getting closer to the hot spot. When they stop at the next checkpoint the sun is casting its own camouflage design of brightness and darkness through the trees onto the road. He picks out two snipers like chameleons against the beige and khaki nettings and wishes he had his own means of defence in the van. He'd asked Rambo to buy him a pistol but it's harder to get a gun in a war-torn country than he'd thought. It seems everyone's after guns.

'This is it, babe,' says Mirren, taking the body armour out of the back of the van.

He pulls his over his head. It belonged to a KIA, Rambo had told him. The thought that a man had died in it still makes him shiver. The last time he wore it, its weight gave him bruises that lasted for days.

Mirren keeps hold of the wheel for the final run into Kharkiv. She's more used to perilous roads from the twists, turns and sheughs of her Scottish Highlands.

'Are you ready?' she asks.

'I've been ready for days.'

He always feels a sense of relief the closer he gets to the action. This close to war the maize fields are deserted, the landscape is ragged and untended, the verges overgrown with wheat grass.

She rolls to a stop at the side of the road.

'What?'

'Rambo gave me a parting gift this morning,' she says with a grin, producing a miniature bag with a marijuana motif. It's the cocktail of drugs that soldiers take on the front line. It's so strong Rambo has warned her of haemorrhages. Matt wants to be the sensible one to Mirren's tender twenty-four but now his nerves are rising he's thirsting for it badly.

'Go on then,' he says, watching her cut two lines on the dashboard.

'Go faster stripes,' she jokes.

One snort and he's lit up like a Christmas tree. The sun is suddenly a passionfruit yellow and the road beats brightly, blueishly. It takes some minutes to adjust to his new reality, to the new confidence burgeoning within him.

As they reach the suburbs of Kharkiv the white concrete apartment blocks are piebald with burn marks. Every telegraph pole they pass is broken. It's only their second trip to the city but it all seems deeply familiar.

Mirren swerves around a huge crater in the dual carriageway. 'Jesus fuck, but the moles are big around here. I'll have to start driving on two wheels!' she chuckles, trying to stay light.

Pasha, the chief of police, is standing outside Saltivka station waiting for them, looking harassed. 'Matt, Mirren, *dobry den*,' he says, shaking their hands. Meeran, he pronounces her name.

A police officer translates for him. 'It's too dangerous to go in,' she says. 'An hour ago, the Russians started shelling.'

'Look, we know the risks but we don't have time to hang around,' explains Mirren passionately. 'We need to get the food to the people and be on our way, ok?'

Pasha raises his voice, unleashing a cascade of words that makes Matt step in.

'Please tell him we'll be fast. All the boxes are ready to go.'

Pasha's chin sways from side to side as he weighs it up. 'Alright,' says the translator. 'But you have to follow fast, yeah?'

Matt and Mirren unload the boxes destined for the frontline soldiers and carry them into the police station. They also hand over the night vision goggles illicitly sent from Poland. Pasha and the translator get into their car while Mirren hops into her seat and revs on the accelerator.

'Here goes. *Fast & Furious,*' says Mirren. Her eyes look wired; her pupils are so big they've colonised her irises.

The police car wails and flashes its blue light. Mirren races after it at eighty mph down the deserted carriageway, ninety mph, a hundred, then presses sharp on the brakes. The speedometer is jumping around madly like a Geiger counter.

'Fuck, I never thought I'd ever be asked to speed by the cops,' laughs Mirren, swerving past another crater.

Matt spots an unexploded shell protruding from the centre of the road. 'Watch out!'

'I'm on it, baby!'

And he can feel the electric thrill of it lighting up his spine as they enter the flattened epicentre, moving down to seventy to avoid the tin paneling and debris blown onto the tarmac. There the smell of burning in the air. Some apartments are pulverised rubble and women are pulling broken chairs out of the concrete for firewood. Their feet are dusty in their frail sandals.

The police car pulls to a halt next to a small nexus of residents. Matt and Mirren have to hand out the boxes fast as the Russians are alert to any movement or gathering. Matt recognises the elderly woman Valentyna from their last trip. She has tears in her eyes and he can't help noticing the smear of dirt on her face from a life led underground.

'Valentyna says "May the blessed angels protect you,"' the translator tells him. 'All the aid workers are too scared to come here but you.'

As if to prove her words a rocket hits a building no more than a mile away, reverberating through Matt's body, making every particle of him shrink.

'Shit,' shudders Mirren.

The blackness blooms in the sky. Pasha is agitated, gesticulating for them to get into their van. They've only just set off when another bomb booms. The police car screeches to a halt by a hospital building. Pasha runs out, hunched from fear of a bombfall, and beckons for Matt and Mirren to join him. Inside the hospital they sit down on the grey plastic chairs by the entrance. Mirren puts on her sunglasses, trying to obscure everything around her. Matt texts his contact Richard to let him know they're delayed in Kharkiv. An unconscious man is stretchered past them. Matt prays that no injured children are carried in. He's fragile enough about not being able to see his own kids and keeps visualising their features in the face of every child he meets.

There's a brief explosion in the distance.

'That one's outgoing,' says Mirren who can always decipher the difference. 'Ukrainian.'

Sometimes he envisages himself joining a foreign battalion to fight on the front line. How could he not after listening to Rambo's swashbuckling tales of fighting hand-to-hand with the Chechens on the Belarusian border. 'Always aim for the body like they're heavyweight boxers,'

Rambo had said, illustrating his moves on Matt's torso. But Rambo was always pouring cold water on his dreams. 'You'd be a bullet magnet,' Rambo had told him, shaking his head at Matt's six-foot-three frame. 'A sniper's wet dream.'

After the bombardment dies away Mirren insists on leaving. Pasha is again disgruntled but Mirren won't back down. This is the Mirren who Matt admires. She's never discouraged or disheartened and, as much as he gets frustrated by her, he finds himself in awe of how local leaders, even the most misogynistic, bow to her will.

They jump into their van and follow the police car. A mile later it stops at a Ukrainian front line and Pasha gets out. He seems calm and authoritative now, chatting to the soldiers.

'Come, come,' a young soldier in an oversized uniform urges Matt, wanting to show him something.

'Sure.'

They crunch over a factory yard full of empty cartridges. A curious smell is lodged in his nostrils like a sickly sweet barbecue. The soldier proudly leads him under an archway to a badly-damaged Russian tank. The rubber round its wheels has burnt away to reveal its massive metal teeth. But as Matt moves his gaze upwards he suddenly realises a dead Russian soldier is protruding through the hatch. It doesn't look human. The soldier's melted black chest is welded to the tank as if he is part man, part machine; a cyborg. Half his skull has been blown away, revealing what looks like a mass of white connected wires. Matt's never seen the intricate mesh of a human brain before. He can see the soldier's profile, his nose, his ear, all perfectly intact. Flies are swarming around it, huge indigo bluebottles feasting, growing plump on what little remains of the charred flesh, and the drone of them makes him dizzy on top of the stench.

The young soldier smiles at him. 'Russkiy. Russian.' He hands him what looks like a weapons manual written in Russian.

'Yes, yes. Very good.'

He feels his stomach lurch again and turns away, hurrying back to the roadside. Mirren is posing on the back of an armoured jeep with an RPG in her arms.

'Go on! Take a photo of me!' she shouts out to him.

The soldiers cheer along with her as Matt takes the snap.

'You and her?' a soldier asks. 'Together?'

Mirren looks at Matt and there's an awkward pause. 'We're still trying to figure that out, aren't we?'

Matt doesn't want to answer. 'We'd better get going.'

He returns to Pasha and shakes his hand, explaining they are behind schedule.

'*Dasvydaniya*, Matt.'

'*Dasvydaniya*.' Matt finds the Russian stick in his throat. He'll never understand the complexity of the region.

He and Mirren walk back to the van across the crumbling road full of dark tank tracks. Inside, she empties her pockets to show him her haul of battlefield treasures, including an RPG case.

'Are you ok?' she checks. 'You look like you've seen a ghost.'

'No. Not a ghost.'

He can feel tremors in his chest again. In the side mirror he can spot the cabbage-shaped plume from a Grad on a distant hilltop, and his heart feels like it is growing uncontrollably inside him. Beside him Mirren intuitively prepares fresh lines on the dashboard.

He bows his head to the powder and the scent of almonds fills his nostrils. As he looks up, Mirren is staring at him. 'Here,' she says, leaning over and kissing him on the lips.

He has a sudden flash of recall of how calm he'd felt strolling with Yulia, her languorous smile, her cool white blouse, but it seems days and miles away, a disappearing peace time memory, and he knows that tonight on the road to Izium when he lays his sleeping bag down in the tight space at the back of the van, he will cling on to Mirren's young skin and pound and thrash inside her like he is fighting a demon because he is bound to her by blood and, inside, he knows Yulia could never follow him to these places, and he's destined to stay with Mirren until the madness works its way out of him.

Mirren drives. Out of the corner of his eye he can see one of the fat flies buzzing in the corner of the windscreen. He quickly flattens it with his knuckles before Mirren starts freaking. It leaves an irradiant smear of blood and tiny yellow guts on the glass.

They pass a hotel 'Adonis' which has two large artillery holes down its side.

'Fancy checking in tonight?' jokes Mirren. 'I've heard the breakfasts are to die for. And, look, it has great ventilation.'

The evening sun is ricocheting through the trees as they return to the countryside. Mirren prattles on about the seafront hotel in Odesa while he gazes out towards a dark puff of smoke above a hilled copse. He tries to think of Yulia in the serenity of the park, face up to the sun, palms out in blissful submission, but she flits away, flickering in and out like the sinking sun through the firs. All he can see is the cartridge-ridden ground and the sight of blood like red borscht pooling on the concrete. The smell of the soldier is not leaving him.

THE PARTICULARITIES

It was my third week on the street when I began to follow
the right path. The days were slipping into September and
the rumpled grey skies were casting a blue breath on the
mountains. The leaves of the nearby cherry trees were
coning in on themselves like the shoulders of the elderly. It
was a mercy it was dry and I could sleep comfortably at
night under the vaulted arches of a church doorway. I'd
learnt the art of pulling my sleeping bag around my face
without suffocating myself, so by morning I'd be lying there
curled just like the beech leaves around me, bunched as
Cuban cigar. At seven, the priest's housekeeper would
toddle over in her sturdy slippers with a cup of tea and a
microwaved scone that was hotter than hellfire in the
middle.

'There you go,' she'd say and, even if it was blowing a
gale, she'd add 'Not a bad morning at all,' for she saw it as
her Christian duty to deliver good cheer.

As soon as the sun climbed with pink shyness behind the
cloud a strange man with a toothy grin like a permanent
gnaw would show up, lumbering on two prosthetic legs,

and start to remove the thick green moss on the sandstone walls circumferencing the church. It was a particularly futile task as the moss left behind a ferrous stain that resembled the Turin Shroud, but I didn't like to say as he was clearly on a mission for the glory of god and relished being out in the open air. He told me he'd had a brain injury which explained it all and I guessed he was expecting me to divulge a similar weakness behind my own predicament, but my injury was quite, quite different. It was spiritual, pertaining to my past.

On this one morning, to get my cold muscles going, I went on a dander, meandering under the calcite skies. I was beginning to love that ambiguity of autumn – the withering fade against the brambling flare of rosehip red. Down by the Loop River the tattered wild irises were as fragrant as honey-infused melon, and I listened to the arias of water flowing and fluting between the rocks. In the silted shallows a discarded carpet was growing small sprigs of grass through its weave, little bog plants rising up through its shag and, when I looked up, the limens between the warm houses and the nature around me seemed to shiver and disintegrate into moving pixelations as shimmery as the petaled water. It struck me for the first time that the street was my own living room, meaning there were no limits to my existence. And it was incredible how my new life kept revealing more false divisions, because there were no seasons, no timelines and no equinoxes in this world. The only sure rhythm was the pulse of the sun and its bone sister, the moon, and in one day the weather could switch and pitch from winter to summer, from spring to autumn, and I could feel the metamorphosis in every organ of my body and it made me understand that my life wasn't a linear march from birth to youth to age to death, but a constant retracking between all these states, and I could die and be reborn at forty in this febrile fusion.

Once I knew all this I felt sure it was the first step to leaving the streets, although I didn't yet know how. A question kept forming in my mind: 'Is there one big thing in your life you wish you could go back and undo?' A wind began to blow, trying to stir me. Still contemplating, I arrived back at the church wall to the rat-toothed man chiseling away at his chore.

'Are you ok?' he asked, his pink cheeks swollen from the breeze. 'You look very pale.'

I told him I was fine. I've always had a tombal pallor, so much so teachers used to insist I was sick and send me home from school in spite of my protests. When I worked in a pub a group of workmen who came for their breakfast called me 'the ghost' behind my back.

The chiseler took out his flask and shared his tea with me. For the past weeks I'd been relying on the generosity of strangers. He let me sip from his cup and he might have been flirting with me but my own boundaries between the corporeal and spiritual were melting away. At times my body was heavy and earthbound while my mind was gossamer; at other times, my body didn't exist while my mind was replete like a stomach after a meal. The one thing I knew was that a slim ectomorph like myself wasn't built for the streets and I needed to plot my escape.

'Tell me. If there's anything you'd go back and change in your life what would it be?' I asked him.

'That's easy. I'd stay in bed the morning I had my car accident,' he said without missing a beat.

I watched for a minute or an hour as the wind swept the leaves into a neat pile in the corner of the churchyard. The sun burst through with a numinous light and a flotilla of butterflies and bees came along and feasted on the last of the buddleia flowers before leaving. Fragments of autumnal orange glitter skipped with them down the road.

After seeing them eat I went to the bakery across the road where they gave me the sausage rolls they'd failed to sell that day, wrapped up in a white paper bag diaphanous with grease. I offered one to the chiseling man who seemed pleased.

'We're getting there,' he said. 'Though where we're getting I don't know.'

Later he left for the bus stop on his rickety legs, his back bent forward as he moved mechanically, the left foot stepping out with a more extravagant kick than the right. It was so fascinating I mimicked his walk myself, analysing how it worked, but just as I trailed after him he turned and saw me and I stopped, mid action, and waved goodbye at him. I felt guilty but as far as the inventory of bad deeds in my life went it was pretty mild.

The orange sky in the west lit the tips of the streetlights. As night fell and the wind calmed, the whistle and explosion of firecrackers resounded, ricocheting against the walls and bouncing off the gable ends like they were part of a big street party. This country was Halloween crazy and, even though it was five weeks away, the threshold between the dead and living was becoming more and more opaque with every passing day. I vowed to myself I'd be gone from the streets by Halloween.

That night I laid down my cardboard imagining it was a yoga mat. I was always having private jokes at my own expense as it helped cheer me up. The church was one of the few buildings in this whole city to be in darkness and I felt safe in its doorway, hiding in the shadows. I wriggled into my sleeping bag and downed some cheap strong cider I'd bought with the last of a tenner from a passerby.

During the night I woke up with the whispers and low cries of children running round the church grounds and the swish and crack of branches, but I kept my eyes shut and in my drunken haze I wondered if it was ghosts flying about –

the zestful dead wreaking havoc. I could almost feel under the cardboard the smooth indents in the sandstone from the years of passing footfall. I told myself I was lying in some magic portal between past and present and, not long after, I drifted off again.

In the morning I noticed that one of the young cherry trees had been pulled down. The priest's housekeeper was striding towards me in her slapping slippers.

'Did you see the kids who did it?' she asked.

'No, sorry. I was asleep.'

She looked disappointed and I realised I was only tolerated because she saw me as some sort of guard dog sleeping out in a kennel. I backed away from her, aware of my own smell. My sweat was beginning to disturb me these days, a strange mix of blackcurrant, licorice and vinegar. I wondered why the children had left me alone. Perhaps they were frightened of catching a virus. Or perhaps they considered me untouchable in the same way they viewed the statue of the Holy Mary recessed in her niche, me being as pale and bloodless as a Mary myself, only a fallen one, self-vandalised, in need of repair. Then again I was no saint at all and that's what I longed to put right.

The morning was a downy grey spitting the lightest feathers of rain. The chiseler hadn't arrived and I imagined he'd looked at the forecast and decided against coming. I tied my sleeping bag up into a bundle, stashed it next to the sacristy and brought my plate and china cup back to the priest's house, setting it on his doorstep as I did every day. I moved out to the main road. The mountains were misty while the slate roofs merged with the grey-marled sky. When it rained in this city everything was so blurred it was like walking around with bad vision, but I had this new sense that now the sky had finally broken it heralded change and I was poised on the cusp of something big.

The rain was getting heavier and began to uncurl the leaves and glue them flatly to the darkening pavement. The wetness tickled my lips – what a thirst I had on me after last night's cider! I didn't have a coin left in my coat so I drank from the loose folds of a rose resting on a hedge. I drained two roseheads at this garden bar, the water tasting of Turkish Delight, and then drank out of a convolvulus flower. It was like imbibing from a conical paper cup at an office water cooler, flavourless and ice-cold.

I walked on past the butterfly tree, now bare of blossom, its denuded tips curling like burnt-down sparklers. I was starting to feel strange and was wondering if the convolvulus bore a drug in its nectar, some sort of transubstantial elixir. I was a drunken bee zigzagging down the pavement but the streets were changing with me and I kept blinking, trying to reset my vision, but the apartment blocks were peeling away to be replaced by houses, revealing topography from ten, twenty, thirty years ago, the neon lights bleaching and fading. The seasons seemed to be retreating – now it was snowy and the pavement was a toboggan run and now it was spring, the road polka-dotted with white blossom. Two giant trees in the paving stones began to slant away from each other like buckling columns pushed apart by an invisible Samson, all barriers dissolving.

But the strangest thing was that the passersby seemed to recognise me and I knew them all from my past. Not one of them had aged from the last time we'd met. And just then I saw a boyfriend I'd loved with all my heart while breaking his. I turned as I watched him pass, my chest springboarding, and I was on the verge of running after him but knew instinctively I still couldn't give up my freedom for his love, and within seconds he'd disappeared behind a file of successive men and the chance was gone.

And I could tell it was my father approaching from his head of white curls which the cancer never took away, though it took his lungs, and I knew he was on his way to the hospital and I should go with him because I'd neglected him badly when he was dying, but all I could do was call 'I love you, Dad,' and he called back with a smile 'Sure I know.'

There were long legions of people I'd worked with in my life walking past and maybe one or two I'd bitched about to a boss and scotched their chances of promotion.

'Sorry,' I said to a girl whose career I'd wrecked. I'd liked her but had been jealous. I began to understand there was no one big action but many reasons why I'd ended up on the streets.

And then I saw him, that little skittery excitable dog bouncing along towards me and, oh, the wonderful life and power in him, and I felt that piercing pain because he was the only being I'd ever condemned to death without even knowing it. His elderly owner, Harry, was out walking him, and I went back to that day twenty years ago when Harry told me the dog was too wild for him. I knew that Harry couldn't cope so I drove them in my car to the canine shelter. Later I heard that the shelter had destroyed the dog.

'Harry, keep your dog!' I shouted as he passed by.

'What's that?' asked Harry, and he was fading before my eyes.

'Don't send him away!' but I couldn't tell if he could hear my plea.

There was a tickle on my eyelashes, followed by the clink of the bell from the church tower.

'Look, she's coming round,' said a voice above me and I could see the buck-toothed grin of the chiseler and his kind blue eyes kindled by the sun. The clouds were peeling back like wind-ripped petals.

The back of my coat was sopping and I tried to get up, but a woman in a mask and a uniform said 'Whoa, take it easy there. Nice and gentle.'

'I'm fine,' I said, rising, but I still felt woozy. There were goldfish swimming in a puddle nearby me, but they were only orange leaves. 'I think it was the flower.'

The ambulance woman looked at me like I was mad, a little cluster of confused wrinkles above her nose tindering the flames of doubt in her head.

A man wearing a badge for 'Street Outreach' said 'We need to get you off this road before you get the virus.'

'There's a new virus?' I hadn't seen the news in weeks.

'A new wave of it. We're moving you into a nice warm flat where you'll be safe.'

'Are you serious?'

I felt ecstatic. This gruff bearded man was an angel and I could tell from his scarred face he'd dived into the same depths as I had. The ambulance pulled away and the chiseler kicked his way on his teetering legs back to the church. I hadn't even thanked him for helping me, but as I watched him cross the slippery road I caught sight of a car hurtling towards him, and within a terrifying heart-splitting second I could tell he was about to hobble into its path.

'Stop!' I yelled.

He halted just long enough for the car to fire past him, the bumper a mere centimetre away from smashing into his flesh.

He hurried across to the sanctuary of the pavement then turned and waved at me from the church wall, its stains more bloodlike than ever in the rusty sunshine. I was shaking but it felt wonderful that I'd saved him, I'd undone something about to be done and finally put a thumbprint of goodness on this world.

I followed the outreach worker to his van, ready to step through a new portal into a different life. I didn't look back, but I could feel the warmth of the sun shining over the church tower as if trying to anoint me with its light no matter where I would go next.

CLEARBLUE

Nicole was late, she was sure of it. Not that she ever counted the days between periods, but it had been more than a month since she'd seen him. The first time they had sex he said he'd wear protection because he gave blood every month, which sounded very noble, but the second time he asked if they could do it without a condom as it always felt better. She kept remembering his inner rhythm and the way he positioned her limbs across the bed like he'd learnt all his moves from a Tantric 'how to' manual.

She was also late for her BBC recording and the sticky September heat was making her hair curl after spending half the morning straightening it. Not that hair mattered for a radio play. She was playing the part of 'nameless woman passenger' and it struck her ruefully that most of the parts she played these days were nameless. The sign for Blackstaff Studios swung into sight ahead of her. Above it a white contrail rocketed across the blue sky, aiming for the sun.

'Ah, at last, darling!' said the producer, air kissing her. His voice was as smooth as his shining pate.

'Great to see you, Eoin.'

'Look, everyone,' he announced, waltzing her over to the other actors. 'Our genius has arrived.'

The producer was Eoin O'Shaughnessy and his Irish name clashed with his anglicised accent, a vestige from living in London. He would call everyone darling, our genius, our saint or the voice of god, in honeyed tones – then would come the sting.

'Could you do it again, darling?' he asked Nicole after her first take. 'And this time try to make it a little less blah.'

In twenty minutes her two scenes were done and Eoin kissed her goodbye, decanting praise into her ear. In the street she walked past the first chemist she came to, telling herself not to be so paranoid. Of course she wasn't pregnant; it was just the crash diets which had messed up her hormones. She darted into the next chemist, however, and picked up a Clearblue. It was the first pregnancy test she'd purchased in her twenty-nine years and the price was extortionate. She flirted with a cheaper brand, but it seemed like an occasion to go with the best.

The chemist in the white coat at the cash desk lowered her voice as if talking of something serious like cancer.

'I'll give you a bag for that, no cost,' she murmured, slipping the Clearblue into the plastic. 'I'm sure you don't want everyone knowing your business.'

Nicole had met Jim, a sound engineer, three years ago and had liked him, but lost touch, so she was happy when he befriended her on Facebook. It wasn't so easy to meet guys live these days. The last time she went up to two handsome men in a bar they'd asked suspiciously 'Are you doing this for a bet? Did your friends put you up to this?' Both guys had girlfriends but added patronisingly 'Fair play to you though for trying.' She'd decided from then on to only meet men online.

Jim was older than her and had two kids with a former partner, but was quick to let her know he was single, and replied to her messages with heart emojis. She was the first one to initiate a meeting by proposing a drink in Belfast. In person he was as hip as she'd recalled, rocking an inside-out t-shirt and jeans so ripped they looked like they'd been vandalised by a jealous lover. He was tall, smiley and retained a hint of punk rebellion in his quiffed hair. He was easy to chat to and chilled and, though he let slip a few mentions of conspiracy theories and the Illuminati, she overlooked it. He said he'd made pasta with puttanesca sauce for his dinner, but she thought he said Putinesque, after the Russian leader, and they laughed together. She felt so comfortable with him she even fessed up to being a heater-upper instead of a cook.

After the bar she invited him back for a drink. At first they sat on her sofa with their gin and tonics while he set his mobile phone between them and played her old tracks from the past. It seemed that to him a drink only meant a drink, when everyone in the entire universe surely knew it meant more.

Finally she decided to come straight out with it. 'Why don't we do some kissing in my room?' she asked, and he looked shocked.

'I don't know. Maybe. Let me just think ...'

'What's to think about?' she replied, wondering if he was still in a relationship with his ex.

'You're right. I don't need to think,' he smiled. 'Let's go then.'

She remembered from that night he'd had a nice cock, his foreskin wide open like a mouth saying 'oh' in surprise. And she remembered him saying 'I'm just a little boy,' turning his earnest blue eyes on her, letting her understand she wasn't to expect anything of him or to hurt him. The sweet childlikeness of it surprised her.

Across the street from the chemist, she spotted her friend Caroline. They decided to go to Clements and took their coffees to a table outside, squeezing the last of the orange sunshine out of the afternoon before it disappeared behind a high-rise. Caroline was still trying for a baby with her partner Phil and was fresh from tests at the hospital that morning. The doctor had said to Caroline with a wink 'Bet it's not you. Bet it's Phil's weak sperm, eh?'

'Ha. Did you tell Phil that?' Nicole asked.

'No way – Phil would go batshit! He thinks I'm the issue.'

Nicole was an ear to cry into for all her girlfriends, but here she was with a pregnancy test in her bag. She was tempted to pour her heart out yet Caroline would hardly be thrilled to hear about a pregnancy at the first go without a condom. Fertility envy they called it.

Nicole decided instead to stick to her usual lighthearted role and tell a funny story about an acting gig. A few days ago she'd arrived at a Lewis Carroll festival on a hangover to discover that the only costume left was Tweedledum with a ginger wig. Tweedledee with a blonde wig she could have handled but Dum was a step too far and, what was worse, the wire costume nearly garotted her. Caroline laughed along, her dark red curls quivering over her forehead like cherry blossom. Nicole's lowly acting career at least provided a source of mirth. Why would you want success if it lost you the ability to make your friends laugh?

At a neighbouring table a toddler with a monobrow and a crisp fragment dimpling his cheek squawled in his pushchair. Nicole tried to ignore him while Caroline continued with her conception chronicles.

'I really hope the baby thing works out for you,' Nicole told her.

She kept thinking of a lesbian couple she knew who had recently ordered sperm from a catalogue. Apparently the man they'd chosen had a history of heart trouble in his family, but his photo as a baby was so cute they couldn't resist him. It was mad thought Nicole. Everything boiled down to looks in the end. Choosing a baby was no different from choosing a man on Tinder.

Back at her apartment she waited. A clear horizontal blue line appeared, but it was no problem as that just proved the test had worked. 'Blue is for boys' kept passing through her mind.

A second blue line was so pale she wasn't sure it existed. She shook the stick like it was a thermometer but didn't know why. Next she arced it through the air like it was a magic wand – abracadabra, you're pregnant, you're not, look away, look back.

This time the blue was distinct and her heart nearly split through her throat.

Blue.

Blue.

Blue.

Blue.

She knew she was in trouble. As her grandmother used to say 'If you burn your arse, you have to sit on the blister.' Oh Christ! She thought of her aunt who was a 'Taliban' Presbyterian and would label her the devil incarnate. And what would her mum say? 'I'm not looking after it,' would probably be her first words. And, more to the point, what would Jim say? He was already devoted to his two children. How much devotion did he have to spare? But did she even want him involved when she'd already frozen him out on Facebook? How would she keep up her acting career with a baby in tow?

A text came through on her phone. It wasn't from Jim, but Eoin thanking her for her work on the play.

'Thanks, Eoin,' she replied but her phone autocorrected to 'Thanks, Oink.' She started to laugh.

The second date was when things had begun to go awry. She'd already noticed something strange about his Facebook posts.

'Jim, why do so many foreign girls comment on your posts?'

'Uh, right.' He coloured a little. 'When I got drunk I used to scroll through girls and friend them but I don't do that anymore.'

Later he told of how a Russian woman had paid for him to fly to Italy for a holiday, and all Nicole could think of was a gigolo. It didn't help that she was providing the gin and tonics and, although she was hardly lavishing a fortune on him, it was a 'sign'. Everything was a sign in dating.

'Why aren't you on Twitter?' she asked.

'Oh, well, I was, but I was shadowbanned for my posts about the deep state,' he admitted.

He seemed to think he was the Julian Assange of Belfast, and it freaked her a little. On the topic of state cover ups he showed her a fuzzy video of Jeffrey Epstein abusing a girl who was tied to the ground. Afterwards she wished she hadn't seen it. She was feeling like an interrogator and dropped the questions, but then that was worse as his voluntary statements, such as being an anti-vaxxer, revealed even more. When he stayed for the night he tossed and turned in her bed for hours and laughed it off, telling her 'I like to move around in bed as much as possible to burn off calories.'

The third time they met he took an hour off from working on a film set and arrived in the afternoon with his van full of sound equipment. He joined her in her room for some loving, mentioning that the producer was paying him a full day's salary.

'It's like I'm being paid to have sex with you!' he exulted.

As he left he talked of meeting up again.

'Y'know, at the start I thought sex would be awkward with you,' he said, scanning her face, 'but it turned out to be really good.'

A few days later he messaged her on Facebook to meet up again and she didn't bother answering, but he messaged her the next day and the next, and before she knew it she'd left it too late to answer. Without meaning to, she was ghosting him. She didn't open his messages but the first half of every first line was always visible to her.

Nicole, why won't you answer my ...?

I don't think you're being fair at all ...

His annoyance surprised her as she hadn't thought he was that into her. She knew she was being mean but she didn't trust herself to reply in case she weakened and gave in to another date. They called men like him boomerangers as they always came back for more.

After guilting her didn't work he tried a different tack.

I watched you in your play last night ...

She knew it was a lie. He was just trying to manipulate her into answering.

She put the pregnancy stick aside and looked out of her window. The sky was still blue but for a series of white cloud ripples in the shape of a thumbprint as if god had put his seal of approval on the world. She remembered she had work to do. She'd promised to record a scream for a friend's stage play, so she sat down at her laptop and opened the recording link but couldn't stop thinking of him, realising she hadn't had a message from him in a week. She could almost smell his aftershave – he wore it so liberally he spread his scent everywhere like a crop sprayer.

She looked up his Facebook page. Three minutes ago he'd posted a selfie, posing with a wad of rent money for his landlord, smiling coyly into his own phone. In spite of everything she still found him red hot.

'*Oh mi amore, mio principe!*' went one of the comments from his foreign female fan club and it made her nauseous. There was another pic of him with his arm round his kids, looking happy. This time a tenderness suffused her.

Oh no, the ellipsis was dancing across her screen – he'd clearly spotted her on messenger. She was about to close it down when she caught sight of the first line.

Fuck you for ignoring me, bitch ...

Oh god, she whispered and tried to compose herself. Surely he was just letting off steam, but she couldn't handle it. She could block him but he still had her phone number.

I know you are reading this ...

She started up the recording.

Only one scream was needed for the play but she decided to give her friend a choice; one with passion, one with horror, one with irony – the voice of a legend, darling, she told herself, mimicking Eoin's voice. Yet once she opened her lungs and let the air in she found she couldn't stop. Scream after scream after scream unfurled from the depths of her and she was sure her neighbours could hear her, this mad girl going insane in her own apartment, carrying the child of someone who freaked her out, and she wondered if they'd phone the police as she looked out to the bone-white cloud waving in a sky that was sea blue.

Blue.

Blue.

Blue.

Blue.

ERIN

It was the start of spring and the early frosts whitened the roofs till the sun rose. Erin was up early to shower, patting her skin in the faint hope that by some miracle the lump might have decoalesced during the night. It wasn't sore but it was tender to the touch, the way a fading bruise might feel. Although she hadn't slept more than a few hours she wondered why she felt so awake. Perhaps when your body experienced an intimation of death it went into overdrive? This past week waiting for the appointment there'd been no sleep in her. She brewed coffee and was about to pour in milk when she paused, remembering a story on the oestrogenic effects of dairy. It was hard to stay away from Google even though, for all she knew, she'd be fine. Go ahead, live a little, she told herself, tilting in the milk. And next time add some whiskey, she laughed. She stood by the window noticing how the geranium on the sill was beginning to open its purple petals. Beyond it she could see the passersby on the street raising their blanched snowdrop-white faces to the morning sun.

As soon as she arrived at the Royal she washed her hands in antiseptic and joined the queue at reception. The waiting room was vast, bigger than A&E, full of orange plastic chairs attached to the floor. Most of the women were older, all neck scarves and flat heels. At thirty-nine she was one of the young cool babes. Nearly everyone had someone with them. Husbands, partners, sisters, friends, daughters. She would have invited her mother but it was a long way to come from Portrush. The husbands were silent, shuffling their feet as if they'd wandered into some feminist meeting and had nothing to add to it.

'Erin White?' a nurse called out.

Erin followed her along the corridor to a set of white cubicles. The last time she'd been in a cubicle was to try on clothes, but now there were no mirrors and, instead of a sheer satin blouse, she was putting on a plain pastel blue gown. As she changed, she could hear the whirrs and clunks from down the corridor. The nurse led her into a small room dominated by a tall white machine. At first sight it reminded her of some giant presser or a vice belonging more to a factory than a hospital.

'The radiographer will take a few images. It'll only take a tick,' the nurse said reassuringly.

Erin worked as events manager for the Irish Cultural Centre on Fountain Street. She scheduled book readings, music events, panel discussions, political debates. She was one of the few Protestants in the office and made sure she booked events that didn't follow the usual Irish Catholic tilt. She was in the middle of emailing a musician when the call came.

'We need to discuss the biopsy results with you as soon as possible,' the voice said. 'Could you come in and see us tomorrow at ten?'

The busy office backdrop became invisible to her.

'Yes, of course. That means bad news, doesn't it?'

'I'm in appointments, so I'm afraid I don't know the details but everything will be discussed with you tomorrow.'

Erin unconsciously rose, picked up her bag and left her desk. She went down in the lift but by the time she reached the exit there was a mizzle in the air as fine as fairy dust and she wished she'd brought her coat. She breathed deep, waiting for her heart to reemerge in its rightful place and resume its normal rhythm. The pavements were lined with skinny trees, their sparse branches uplifted in little candle flames of fresh buds like a menorah.

She phoned her mother to tell her the news.

'Don't you fret,' said her mum, her voice as soothing as an emollient. 'We'll face this together no matter what.'

The words 'no matter what' chilled her. Oh Christ, it was just a phrase, stop imagining the worst, she told herself. You'll be grand. She took the lift back up to the office, ready to return to organising events, visualising months into the future, and it struck her that it had been a long time since she'd lived in the present. Only two weeks ago she'd been booking a holiday to India for the autumn. If friends called and invited her to do things spontaneously she usually turned them down. It seemed her job had seeped into the way she lived her life. She sat back down at her desk.

Niamh who worked opposite said 'Thought you were on an early lunch there.'

'No. Just had to make a private call.'

'Oooh. Go on, tell us, who is he?'

No one,' Erin grinned, thinking how ludicrous Niamh was.

'Don't tell us then,' went Niamh a little huffily.

Erin longed to tell someone and feel the caress of sympathy, but it had to be the right person. Sure, Niamh had once mentioned that she kept her face deliberately expressionless to avoid the ageing process. How could a girl like Niamh understand what goes on beneath the skin?

She went with her mother to meet with a consultant on an ice-cold, brumey day with a silver coin of a sun. The consultant showed her the images of her breast against the black from different angles. He pointed out a couple of dark masses, but could have been showing her an ultrasound of a baby in a womb for all she could really tell. The main point was the cancer was only stage 1(b) and the prognosis was good.

'1(b)? But I've always been an A student,' she said to her mother to make her smile. The only way to cope with illness was to laugh at it, especially now it wasn't fatal.

'In my estimation the operation should remove the cancer and you won't require chemo,' said the consultant, 'but we'll make a decision on that at a later date.'

It was almost unbelievable to think of her breast being removed. This amputation. When she tried to picture herself naked, her mind blocked it. She barely registered the consultant's question about reconstruction, but pulled herself together, recalling someone at work who had taken a long time to heal from the skin grafts.

'No, thank you.'

'Are you absolutely sure?' Erin's mum checked, her dark eyes scouring her face.

'No problem. You can always consider reconstruction later,' the consultant said, pen poised on his pad, ending the discussion.

The days moved on and every morning the skies were ruffled like coconut flakes. The moment before the sun rose, a lavender light was achingly cast through the blinds into Erin's room. A few days later the letter arrived informing her she was scheduled for a mastectomy on her left breast. 'You won't require chemo,' he'd said, but what were the percentages? A five percent chance? Ten? More? With coronavirus, there had been percentages galore: chance of dying, chance of needing a ventilator, chance of having long covid, but when it came down to it you always fancied your chances at the age of thirty-nine. Percentages reminded her of school. She'd always been in the top five percent academically. 'A hundred percent,' was the way she sometimes answered a question in the office in lieu of saying yes. She would always back herself to win.

She kept thinking of Hugh, imagining his reaction. They'd been together two years, but broke up six months ago when she found out he was on Tinder. A friend had showed her his profile one day. He hadn't even bothered concealing it with a fake identity. She couldn't get over the notion that he'd kept saying 'I love you' to her while seeing other women. Those three words might have been hollow to him but meant everything to her.

She missed Hugh's physical presence; the way his body felt as strong and grounded as a tree trunk, his huge boughs of arms enfolding her. His beard was soft moss to the touch. Perhaps because her own body was weakened, she missed his even more. She could still visualise his hands on her breasts, cupped as a climber's as he moved down her body. Every man she'd been with had admired them. It was hard to lose the best of herself, almost ironic for cancer to attack her beauty now she was single.

The night after the letter came she woke up in a hot sweat after dreaming the surgeon was cutting into the right side instead of the left. She went downstairs for water, noticing the snow duveting the roofs. Outside, the cars were white as though the sky had covered them in sheets. When she tasted the tap water it was icier than it had ever been. She walked out into the snow, the heat of her feet making the wet run into her slippers. Her body was still warm. The lump was right above her heart and she wondered if her heart would be colder without the flesh to protect it. She wondered if the reason the lump had prospered was because of her rage at Hugh.

At work Niamh had her usual lunchtime picnic assembled on her desk – gourmet gherkins in dinky tubs, charcuterie, gluten-free rye bread, carrot sticks and tzatziki. Erin brought out the Belfast bap she'd bought in the Spar that morning. She'd been so preoccupied she'd forgotten to buy bread to make her own sandwiches.

'What *is* that?' asked Niamh.

'Tuna and sweetcorn.'

'Looks heavy on the mayo,' commented Niamh with a moue of disapproval.

Oh god, Niamh was right, she should have been putting the best of food into her body right now, preparing it for surgery. Even so, it was irritating how Niamh envisaged that a perfect diet might protect her from illness for ever. Homemade bread and a celery stick were no guarantee of immortality.

'Parmesan crisp?' offered Niamh, holding out the bag.

She pronounced it Parmejan in some kind of pretentious Italian homage that made Erin cringe. Hummus and chorizo were regularly butchered on her lips.

'Tacheeky?' asked Niamh, holding out the tzatziki.

After lunch, Erin went to see her boss, Helena. Helena possessed a confidence that filled the corridors and almost blew the rest of the staff into the walls with it. She exuded good health to such an extent it was intimidating.

'How can I help you?' asked Helena.

'I need to book four weeks off work for an operation,' Erin said quickly to head off any questions.

'That's fine and of course you can have time off. I'll just need a photocopy of your surgeon's letter.'

'Oh.' Erin realised how naive she was not to bring proof. 'Sorry, I'm just forgetting everything these days. But don't worry, it's not brain surgery.'

'I think you'd need a little more than four weeks for that,' smiled Helena.

Kindness radiated from Helena but she left a long pause and Erin knew she had to say something.

'It's just ... I'm keeping it quiet but it's breast cancer.' She felt the blood rushing into her cheekbones. The tears teetered, but she held it together.

'Oh no. So sorry to hear that,' said Helena, her face clouding.

'It's fine. They've caught it early. With any luck, it will all be gone with this op.'

'Well, let's hope so. I won't say a word to anyone, but will you tell Niamh to look after your events while you're away?'

'Yes. Of course,' she said, already knowing she couldn't tell Niamh the truth.

Helena squeezed her arm at the door, just a light gesture of sympathy, but the emotion rushed to Erin's eyes again. She could see the sun in the atrium and how the snow was melting, turning translucent at its edges; she could almost hear the cracks and drips of it. She walked downstairs, opened the fire exit and followed a bird track in the snow, its feet in the shape of an arrow. It felt like a message. It led her into the street where the snow slid from a car windscreen as if a hand had pulled away a white tarpaulin. At that moment, she decided to tell Niamh she was taking four weeks off to take care of her mother.

She felt a tiny stab in her chest. Sometimes she kept reliving the sensation of the long thin needle from the biopsy. She wondered if her body was anticipating the touch of the surgeon. A new idea was growing within her, a conviction that she needed to make the most of herself before her surgery.

She spotted him on Tinder. She was swiping so fast, her finger on such a groove, she almost missed him. Jesus Christ, but there were some unattractive guys online, she thought, noticing one with a roll of fat round his neck like a travel pillow. It was important to her to choose well. She wasn't going to go out with any old 'pig in a poke' as her mum would call it. But when she saw this man – his name was Declan – she knew he was the one and it felt like belated revenge on Hugh. She wondered why she hadn't done this months ago.

Declan was thirty-seven and pale, all tubercular cheekbones with thick black hair and huge dark eyes under expressive eyebrows. A tattoo was creeping out from under his t-shirt. He lived two point two miles away, and the accuracy of the reading made her smile. He was the only man she clicked on because she didn't want the stress of having a choice. Immediately he clicked back to show he liked her too. Her mum's words about how she'd met her father swam into her mind. 'We just clicked,' was the expression she'd used.

How are you doing? Erin wrote in the chat box.

Good – you look great.

So do you. That tattoo is cool.

Are tattoos you're thing then? Do you have any?

Bad grammar, should be your, she automatically said to herself, then dismissed it as she needed to type back fast.

No, I don't have any myself.

She thought of her own body and was overtaken by an image of sutures and pink shiny scars, but quickly shunted it out of her mind.

But yours is sexy ...

Declan wasn't a drinker so they agreed to meet up for a walk on a Tuesday evening. The weather was milder and the catkins were just inching their way out of the silver birch at the end of her road. Every tree was burgeoning with red buds – it was as if spring had painted the tips of their fingernails in preparation for a night out on the town.

Erin nervously applied her own red blush to her cheeks. Her lipstick was 'plum beautiful' and, after applying it, she blotted her lips with tissue. The last thing she wanted was to be like Niamh whose red lipstick sometimes leaked onto her teeth like a bad case of gingivitis.

She set out to meet him at the blueing edge of the evening. Along her street, living room lights illuminated figures hunched over their laptops. She guessed everyone was looking for love or cheap goods – or perhaps good cheap love, she chuckled to herself, trying to dispel her nerves.

When she saw Declan standing outside St Anthony's Church he wasn't as tall as she'd imagined, but he had an angularity of jaw and cheekbone as if chiseled by a sculptor to perfection. She loved the whiteness of his skin within its frame of black hair. His manner was relaxed enough to put her at ease, yet confident enough to make her edgy.

'I'm off to London next Monday,' Declan told her. 'Playing gigs round the Irish bars with a trad band. Then off to Switzerland for a tour.'

'Glad I caught you then,' she smiled, 'before you're off on your drugs, sex and trad tour.'

'Ha, the rest of my band are like altar boys! But, seriously, I thought this week would be a window to meet up.'

'It's a window for me too,' she said, thinking that Monday was the morning of her operation.

'Which way do you want to go?'

'Take me in your direction,' she said, aware of her own subtle meaning.

Declan lived in one of the new social housing estates off Global Avenue that had been designated as fifty percent Catholic. As they entered, huge banners bearing images of trees proclaimed 'Families Growing Together' and 'Strong Roots make Beautiful Leaves'. The imaging made her realise uncomfortably that there was a new plantation in the east.

'Look at all the social messaging,' she said, finding it oppressive. 'One Community, One Love' a banner said and another declared 'Mine, Yours, Ours' with a red tick beside 'Ours'.

'I don't even notice it. We're colonising the east!' exulted Declan. The words slipped out before he could stop them, and her silence told him she'd stumbled on the tripwire. 'Shit! Sorry. I thought from your name, but you're a Protestant, aren't you? I didn't mean that.'

'It's ok,' she said, not wanting it to get between them.

'It's just the sort of stuff I say to my republican pals. To please them.'

'It's grand.'

'Do you still want to come in?'

She smiled at him. 'Course I do.'

As they reached his front door, a chihuahua leapt up onto the windowsill to bark at her.

'Don't mind Tyson,' said Declan. 'He may be tiny but he thinks he's a guard dog.'

Tyson growled in the hallway and made feints at her ankles.

'No, Tyson! Leave!' shouted Declan. 'He takes a while to get used to you, but he'll let you come to him in a bit.'

'Like most men in my experience,' joked Erin.

'Not me. I move fast,' laughed Declan, pulling her into him by the waist. After they'd kissed, he whispered 'Want to come upstairs?'

In the bedroom Declan used the toes of his left boot to pull off his right, almost tripping over himself in his eagerness. Erin could feel the beat of her blood as she undressed, the adrenaline making her fingers unbiddable as she wrestled with the buttons. For quickness, she pulled her blouse over her head.

'Can you take it off?' she said of her bra and he unhooked it easily.

'Beautiful,' he said, touching her, taking in her whole body. 'You're perfect.'

Perfect. The word was poignant and she curved her hands around his to make him cup the flesh, touching her breasts herself. They were as soft as freshly risen soda bread, just the faintest blue of a vein beneath, culminating in a plump pinkness. She wished time would stop still, but the moment was too evanescent to hold.

She could feel him hard against her thigh and she pulled down his jeans. His cock quivered, almost sensing her fluids, and they fell onto the bed. She was so hot for him, the pinkest, tenderest parts of her skin were scalding. To get closer to him she knocked her elbow against his ribs, hit her skull against the headboard, but she didn't even feel it and reached out blindly for him, their bodies eliding. She could feel a prickling in her left breast and wondered if it would haunt her after the loss like a phantom limb. Is this what it will be like, she asked herself.

An hour later as she was leaving Declan's house Tyson danced round her feet, nostrils dilating, looking puzzled as to why her scent was commingled with his master's.

'Shall I contact you when I'm back from my travels?' asked Declan.

'I'd honestly rather leave tonight as a one-off, if that's ok with you.'

'Oh, that's fine, that's fine,' he said and she couldn't tell if it was relief or disappointment.

'But tonight was so great,' she went on, trying to soften the moment, 'and, look, give me your email and I'll get you a gig through my work.' With his email she could still pretend they were leaving things open.

Outside, the weather had changed. The long forecast Atlantic storm was starting to stir. The banners were slapping against the lamp posts. Shadow branches were undulating on a white wall, reminding her of the beautiful dark briars from fairy tales. On the main road Union Jacks were shaking in excitement. She tied her scarf tighter and the crook of her arm brushed against her chest. Tonight was some send off, she told herself, and she grinned, happy to have immortalised herself in her memory, though in time she'd have to get used to the next incarnation. Oh, the vanity of her when the main point was that the cancer would be gone.

She passed a sycamore tree which was uttering husky sighs. The wind-filled plastic bags were caught in its boughs, beating back and forth like party balloons wielded by children. The spring leaves made the fizzing sound of champagne, the tips of the twigs clapping together in applause, and a wind chime jingled, growing louder and louder.

MAGHABERRY

The sun is flickering and the cameras are flashing as she's led out of Laganside Courts. She could cover her head with her jacket, as criminals do, sneaking out in shame, but she refuses to succumb. Photos of her have already adorned the papers and one or two more won't make a difference. The police van is parked next to a wall purple with clematis. Bees are suckling on the sugary stamens, quivering with delirium.

The press are still calling out to her as she climbs in. She sits down on the black vinyl seat and the light darkens as the doors clunk shut. She lets herself breathe, lets her mouth fall open. It's odd to be in her Sunday best in the back of a van that smells of antiseptic wipes and prisoners' sweat. She straps on the seatbelt, her suit slipping on the vinyl as the van turns away from the court.

'Alright back there, Roisin?' asks the police officer, Eddie, through the grill.

'Grand.'

She used to work with both Sonya at the wheel and Eddie in the passenger seat. She wonders if she'll ever get accustomed to being on the other side of the law.

'The judge was awful hard on you there,' comments Sonya.

'Only because you're police.' Eddie shakes his head. 'If you were Jo Bloggs you'd have got four years, out in a year and a half.'

'Like, it's not as if you did a hit and run.'

It was true they were making an example of her. Ten years, the judge had said, and the pronouncement was a stone dropping through her body, while sobs and joyful shouts rang out from Trevor Gilmour's family. There was triumph and it was only natural they hated her for taking the life of the man they loved. Unforgivable, Roisin says to herself, but even as she says it she feels numb. These days words are just sound.

The van heads into the deep foliage of June.

'Going the scenic route,' chirps Sonya.

They speed along the steep rises and plummets of the Hillhall Road. The same road is always flooded in winter. She can hear branches caress one side of the van, the feathery slap of the leaves, the shuddering potholes, the gravelly sheughs under the wheels. How she'd loved being out on these roads in unmarked cars, cornering high-speed bends as she chased after offenders. She'd been blessed with a rare feel for the different cambers, grades of asphalt and inclines. She can sense them now – ha, there are more twists and turns on the Hillhall Road than an Agatha Christie plot. It's stifling in the back, the sun beating down on the van through the gaps in the leaves. The seatbelt is a tight fit, trapping her arms by her sides.

'Eddie, could you open the window please?' she asks.

'Sure thing.'

With the window open, new scents ribbon in from the blackberry flowers in the hedgerows to the sweet peas and deep musky velveteen roses from the gardens. She closes her eyes and lets the air wash over her while Eddie and Sonya chat away in birdlike song from some faraway treetop. It's always easy for her to phase out. Her impaired hearing was a legacy of the 90s when Protestant youths had hurled stones at her school bus. A half-brick had broken through the glass hitting her on the left side of her head. It only affected her badly in echoing spaces, but still had an impact. She could never, for instance, have taken a job in surveillance.

Sonya takes the roundabout exit to bypass Lisburn. Sonya's always too late and heavy on the brakes – you'd think she was after a whiplash claim! One time, Roisin was riding shotgun in a high-speed chase when Sonya sheared the wing mirror off a stationary car. 'Don't mention that in your report,' Sonya had said to her afterwards. Always lying and covering up.

'Hope we're not on riot duty tonight,' Sonya is saying.

'Hope to god not,' agrees Eddie fervently. 'There's bound to be trouble again on the Shankill.'

'What was it like last night?' Roisin asks.

'Oh, you know, the usual,' says Sonya, glancing at Eddie.

Closing down the conversation, thinks Roisin.

'Here, have a Percy Pig.' Eddie passes her a sweet through the grill.

'Thanks.' She's so grateful for any kindness right now.

'Sure, have a few.'

'No. One is fine,' says Roisin. The grill reminds her of feeding time at the zoo.

The flowerbeds outside Hillsborough are arranged in the shape of a royal crown. Very Protestant, she thinks. Geraniums, orange lilies and marigolds neatly sit in baskets hoisted from every lamp post. The van crawls behind a tour bus all the way up Main Street, past the sandstone gates that lead to the castle and gardens. There are hordes of visitors violently pink from the sun – in this country people seem to think you need third degree burns before you can get a tan.

Sonya speeds up over the brow of the hill and, suddenly, the countryside is splitting out of its hedged seams, the tree trunks fringed with fresh green shoots, the sedge overrun and unruly. Branches clatter against the top of the van, fat bunches of green sycamore seeds tapping and scraping like fake nails.

'Jesus, near had my eye out there,' says Eddie, closing his window.

In the distance is the dark green roll of the Dromara Hills and she knows it isn't far now. She looks out thirstily to the last sight of the crooked hawthorn hedgerows, the elderberry flowers frothing and foaming, the tiniest birds looping across the windscreen, dicing with death, while wood pigeons rise out of the fuchsia bushes. Wild rhododendrons flare in the fallow fields, pale heads of wheat, bright yellow rape seed, making her wish she could hold back time, freeze-frame it in this moment. The two officers are oblivious, babbling away lightly, two gods in eternity, aspiring to nothing more than they possess.

'It's my youngest's birthday tomorrow,' Sonya's saying. 'I've told her we're off to Laser Quest. She can't wait.'

'Class. She'll love it.'

'Aye, she'll get to shoot her mother!' laughs Sonya.

She'd always imagined having children herself although her husband Patrick had warned her she was leaving it late. Too obsessed with your career, said Patrick. Maybe she'll be released in four and a half years, if all goes well, but by then she'll be forty-one. Still, isn't it better this way than leaving a small child motherless for so many years?

'Maghaberry' says the sign on the verge. The village shuttles into view, two sparse lines of cottages and new builds. There is a bittersweet scent in the air. She recognises this road from taking other prisoners on the journey and, just like Sonya and Eddie, she'd chatted away in the front seats, regarding the human being behind the mesh as insentient.

'Did you see that on the news last night?' goes Eddie. 'This air ambulance was landing to save a woman's life, only the woman's mate was blown over in the downdraft and killed.'

'Jesus fuck,' chuckles Sonya darkly. 'The Lord giveth and He taketh away alright.'

On the outskirts of the village she sees an elderly man standing hunched like a heron with a long shaggy grey beard. His stillness draws in her eye, speaks to her somehow, symbolising some sort of stoicism. Sonya turns the van towards a huge set of rusty gates. H.M. Prison Maghaberry. The sight of brown brick buildings and perimeter fence topped by barbed wire sinks into the crucible of Roisin's stomach. She notices that in spite of the heat every single window is shut. Jesus Christ. 'The Men Behind the Wire' starts playing in her head as it always does when she sees a jail and she tries to banish it. The Irish republican lies deep in her.

'We're here,' says Eddie, craning round to look at her through the grill.

What, you think I can't tell, she'd like to retort, but doesn't say a word.

The outer gate slowly opens and Eddie pulls the authorisation papers out of his jacket, handing them to a guard. The red and white arm bar lifts and the van trundles in. Roisin takes out her phone and answers her sister's last text message, sending love and kisses. There is nothing from Patrick, although he must have heard the news by now. Not that she is surprised as they're estranged, but a message would have been kind. Doesn't matter – when she thinks back to her marriage all she views it as is a seven-year sentence. Revisionism helps her cope.

'Good luck, Roisin,' calls Eddie as the prison officer opens the van door.

Roisin doesn't reply, glancing up warily at the windows. She doesn't want the inmates to think she's favoured in any way.

The officer takes her into the airy reception where she recites her name, date of birth and address, and paperwork is handed to her, lists of questions about her medical and criminal histories. One section asks about drug use and, though she is clean now, she ticks yes to attending a counselling course. She'll say yes to everything if it means a reduced sentence. The officer searches through her personal possessions and places in a paper bag the few items she can bring to her cell. She has a long wait in a holding cell before she's given a number and her prison kit. As she pulls on her grey trousers, a dandelion seed, some lone emissary from the outside world, floats down from the air onto the chair beside her.

Next she's given her dinner on a tray. The buttered potato is congealed and the dun mince is submerged in a pool of brackish grease. From the dark tea in her mug she deduces that the canteen staff are country folk. 'That strong, a mouse could trot in it,' her mother used to say of the tea the farmers made.

Afterwards she looks out at a pink-tinged daisy in the shortcut grass. It reminds her of the night she crashed, though her memory is blank until the moment of being cut from the car, the shearing sound, the light on the fireman's helmet. Later, she couldn't believe she'd driven nearly all the way to Craigavon. She could believe even less that she'd killed Trevor Gilmour. The photos of the accident showed wild flowers on the grassy banks of the motorway, poppies and giant daisies. Poppies, that's for remembrance, she says to herself, with a vague memory of verse. When the police had arrived at the scene they'd found her wearing her slippers.

A mugshot for her ID card is taken and she tries to smile for it, determined to stay upbeat. She remembers the first day in the force and the wide grin on her photo. She was so proud of being one of the new tranche of Catholic police officers. Her husband and sister had been against her new career, claiming she'd be targeted by paramilitaries on both sides and labelled a turncoat by her family back in Ballymurphy, but she was determined to be part of change.

'So. Do you want to go to the seg unit?' the officer asks her.

'What?'

'The segregation unit. I'm guessing that's what you want.'

'No, I thought I'd go in with the prisoners.'

He seems surprised. 'Well, if you're sure.'

'I'm not sure of anything,' she says, but she knows she has to face the other prisoners sooner or later. She can hardly spend four and a half years in solitary.

A warder with anaemic skin from being locked up all day shows her to her wing. His boots echo on the tiles while her light prison gutties don't make a sound. The electric lights are harsh, the skylights showing a darkening blue. The cell doors are all locked but a low banging starts up against the metal. Cries of 'black bastard!' resound through the landing. Her legs turn light with fear as she's led up the stairs. 'Pig, pig, pig!' chant the women. Her hysteria rises on the screeks and scrakes of their voices, but she tells herself it's no worse than policing a riot with masonry flung at her head and petrol bombs flying. She's used to seeing hate. She wonders if she'll know any of their faces.

'Here you go,' says the warder, opening the cell door.

She can hear a porcine snorting from the adjoining cell.

'A warm welcome you're getting,' the warder says, giving her a rueful smile.

'They'll ...' She makes the sign of throat slitting so the women can't hear her give voice to her trepidation.

The warder gives a light shrug.

'Sure you can hide in here. Sleep well,' he says, closing the heavy door behind him.

No sympathy from him. Not that she can blame him. She killed a man, extinguished his beloved life when he deserved to die quietly, bloodlessly in his bed. In some ways she's glad of her long sentence as she couldn't have lived with herself on a light one.

She takes a pee in the low toilet, then cleans her teeth with a brush that hard her gums bleed. A girl on the other side of the wall is shouting out.

'Peeler cunt!' she can just about make out. The high timbre of the voice evokes an image of a thin angry teenager, the type of wee millie she had to pull from stolen cars and handcuff. She tells herself she can handle such a girl since she's always been the strong stocky type. She turns off her hearing aid and puts it in its box. If only there was a switch with which she could turn off her thoughts as easily. She gets under the light bedding, pulling off her sweatshirt and lobbing it onto the chair. The cell isn't warm, but she knows she will toss and turn on the hot coals of her memories. It's just then that she sees the tiny red Sacred Heart painted onto the white wall next to her bed.

'O most holy heart of Jesus,' she whispers in relief, tracing its outline with her fingers, recalling from her childhood the prayers that helped staunch the stream of words in her head.

The light snaps off and there is total darkness before her eyes adjust to the light from the window. An Alsatian is barking outside. She travels back to the afternoon she kept phoning Patrick. He wouldn't answer her calls and she was getting more and more frustrated. Oh, it was clear to her he was with that woman from Craigavon. He'd said he'd end it with her, but a born liar he was and couldn't be trusted. She worked herself up into a frenzy, imagining their bodies colliding, the way his eyes widened during sex and the sighs of him. Feverishly she tore open the new bottle of whiskey and downed a glass, even though she'd been telling herself to go easy on the liquor. Then, to stop herself shaking, she burst the temazies out of the pack, little jellies the colour of cod liver oil, and swallowed two. The doctor had recently prescribed them and it said on the box 'Do Not Take with Alcohol' but she ignored it. It's the last memory she has before the crash.

A voice shouts out from another cell. She can't hear the words, can't tell if it's directed towards her or another inmate or to the past. Perhaps it's just the way of incarcerated bodies to cry out at night. To rail against the injustice of justice. Soon enough she will find out. She touches the wall at the point where she thinks the Sacred Heart is, the benedictions stirring silently within her. What she needs is protection for tomorrow and to get through all the hours that follow. She keeps visualising the advent calendars she had as a child and recalling how the December days dragged and Christmas never came quickly enough. She feels the cold wall with her fingers and hears the words pour in beads from her lips. 'Protect me, good Jesus, in the midst of danger, comfort me in my afflictions, give me health of body, assistance in my temporal needs, your blessing on all that I do, and the grace of a holy death, so help me god.' Hot tears burst to her eyes and she feels a flood of warmth surging through her fingertips. For the first time today she knows she will get through.

OESTROGEN CITY

It was a lashing down Sunday evening when Grace and I arrived at the Tipsy Bird. It was one of those vast modern bars with jewel-encrusted bird cages tethered to the walls and copious red fabric roses. Grace said it was boho chic, but it wasn't my scene at all. I'm into traditional snug bars, more Presbyterian plain than Cathedral Quarter Oirish. There's nothing more thrilling than sitting in a snug from where they used to plan terrorist attacks.

As we went to a table we noticed the bar was populated with women checking us out in a competitive way. Grace looked fantastic in a red dress while I was less glamorous, as I didn't do dresses, but it was a qualm that could easily be overcome with a bottle of Corona or three. I'd no idea why I always ordered Corona, but it must have been to do with coronavirus trauma.

'What'll it be?' asked the bartender.

Grace surveyed the menu and plumped for a provocatively-named cocktail.

Part of me wondered what the hell I was doing there. It was Grace's idea to go speed dating in the first place because she'd just broken up with her husband and was dying to cheat on him, even if it was only retrospectively. So here we were on a Dump or Date night for 28–42 year-olds which seemed a random age limit, but must have fit some dating algorithm. As a thirty-four-year-old city planner it wasn't easy to meet a guy. Belfast was Oestrogen City. It felt like women outnumbered men two to one, so drastic measures were called for if you wanted to partner up. I'd have even hopped on a bus up to a Ballymena field and hung around for a buff farmer to dander along, but of course I needed a book reader, not a cow breeder. As a city planner you'd have thought I could plan meeting someone, but my private life was chaos.

Naturally, I'd given dating apps a go, but most guys' idea of getting to know you was bombarding you with sexts! Speed dating was almost as retro as going to an Irish matchmaker, but I was convinced it would be easier to filter out the weirdos eye-to-eye than digitally. The thing was, I wanted a man to have kids with, and I'd even started taking Folic Acid in preparation, which might have been a bit premature, but indicated a positive mindset if nothing else. After our first drink, the organiser Olivia, a confident woman with injudiciously slathered eyeshadow, announced 'Welcome to the Tipsy Bird Dump or Date night! All those who signed up, please make your way upstairs.'

The staircase was lined with photos of inebriated birds. There was a robin perched on the salted rim of a giant margherita and a wren sipping from a coupe of champagne. As we walked up I glanced behind me, making eye contact with a blond guy and I sort-of-smiled and he sort-of-smiled back. Upstairs, we perused the available men. Grace had her eye on a tall guy with chest muscles that nearly popped the buttons off his shirt. The blond guy from the stairs was studying his phone, playing it cool. After more drinks Olivia made another announcement. 'Sorry,' she informed us sheepishly. 'We have fifteen women and only five men, but we'll just have to go ahead.'

We outnumbered the men so badly I wondered if we'd have to act like male primates, shaking our posteriors in the air and hooting to attract their attention. I sat down at my table with my dating form. Each date was scheduled to last a brief four minutes and it was up to the men to circulate. My first guy was the muscleman Grace had liked – a builder called Robert.

'Is this your first time at Dump or Date?' I asked.

'Oh, I've been to loads of them,' Robert said. 'Sure, what else would you be doing on a Sunday night but sitting in talking to the walls?'

It seemed he was looking to pass the time rather than find a date. 'Have you ever been married?' I asked him.

'No. I never met the right person, but as a friend once said to me "Know what you are? You're unclaimed treasure."'

We didn't appear to have anything in common other than an appreciation of each other's good teeth.

'Next date!' shouted Olivia. I thought there would have been a bell to let us know that our time was up, but there was a lot of yelling instead. After each man you were meant to dump, friend or date him. I was half-tempted to tell Olivia the verb of friend is befriend and I shouldn't have to deal with such sloppy modernisms, but I let it go. Dump seemed a bit harsh, and friend seemed pointless, so I ticked date.

My next man, Paul, stepped up or rather hobbled. He was wearing a moon boot and held a crutch.

'I hope you have a crutch fetish,' Paul joked as he awkwardly manoeuvred himself into his chair.

'Absolutely. I have a crutch on you,' I said and because he didn't smile I had to spell out my joke. 'A crush on you.'

He still barely smiled. The only question on my mind was what had happened to him, but it seemed too much like highlighting his disability. He sat hiding his speed dating form like he was preventing me from copying his answers in an exam. I was beginning to realise it was the little things that reveal character flaws. He told me he'd come tonight with two female friends he worked with in the civil service. They were both sitting at a table with the blond man which was incredibly strange as if they were interviewing for a threesome.

'Next date!' came the shout and Paul picked up his crutch and hobbled off. I had a hiatus before my next man, so I joined the rest of the women sitting on the sofas. An older woman was recounting her adverse experience of being stood up by a man from Tinder.

'It isn't easy for us girls in our forties, is it?' she said to Grace who seemed furious. Grace is only thirty-five.

'I don't know what I'm looking for,' said a Japanese woman who looked as if she'd arrived straight from her sofa. 'I'm instinctive, but I'll know when I see it.'

Grace and I went to the toilets for an impromptu debrief. The bathroom doors were all distressed wood and the hand dryers were painted a shade of rusting bronze. I couldn't take much more faux decadence, but at least we were alone.

'You know Robert?' Grace confided. 'He's from the same village as me, but I couldn't tell him anything. I don't want everyone at home knowing I'm speed dating.'

The way she talked about it you'd think we were working at a seedy strip joint, but I guessed in the country bible belt she would have been expected to sit in on a Sunday night in her gingham dress, waiting for a gentleman caller.

Downstairs, the dates were in full flow. I returned to my table where my next date was a big guy, Sam. A waterfall of sweat was running down his brow and he kept stabbing the

Bic biro into its holder with a compulsion no doubt related to his habit of throwing snacks down his throat. He'd been a travel agent until covid, and claimed to have started his own company from home, but it seemed suspiciously like code for being unemployed. We talked about travel to pass the time which was stretching way past our allotted four minutes, and a flustered fear grew in Sam's eyes as if he was being cross-examined. It was becoming excruciating and we both looked around for Olivia to move us along, but she'd forgotten about us and was patrolling the other side of the room, leaving us suspended on this needle tip of nervousness.

'Next!' brayed Olivia, and Sam was surprisingly agile as he moved away.

Finally, the date I'd been waiting for all evening. The blond guy arrived like a Force Nine, throwing himself into the seat to make the most of every second. His skin was tight over his cheekbones, making him look youthful, though I guessed he was in his late thirties. Blond hairs jutted from his stubble catching the light and drawing my eye to his lips. I really liked this man. His name was Andor, he told me in a foreign accent with a Belfast twang, and it was his third time speed dating.

'I'm so tired of the same old questions,' he said, glittering-eyed. 'Go on, ask me something new and different.'

This is it, I said to myself. Now or never to impress him. 'Oh, good. I like a challenge,' I said, even though in reality I'd have much preferred an easy conversation. 'Right. What's your ... best ever experience in Belfast?'

Andor was delighted I hadn't asked him anything obvious. 'Great question. I would say ... it's yet to come.' There was a teasing promise in his smile. 'And what about your best experience ever? Not just Belfast, anywhere in the world.'

I knew he was Eastern European, but didn't know from where, so I decided to test him obliquely. 'My best trip ever was to the Tatra mountains. Zakopane.'

He looked surprised. 'You were in the Tatras?' I could see in his eyes he knew I was fishing for his origins and he was contemplating whether to keep it mysterious for now. So much thought in that moving iridic blue!

'Next date!' Olivia bellowed and it seemed like I'd only had one minute with Andor.

'Better go,' he said, smiling. 'Pity. I wanted more.'

He headed to the Japanese woman, but I didn't have time to mourn his departure as my last date had arrived. The guy looked to be well over the age of forty-two, but since you didn't have to furnish any proof, a seventy-year-old could have shuffled in on his Zimmer frame and been welcomed.

Dates finished, I went downstairs with Grace.

'That bloody Andor,' she raged. 'He was so rude and all I did was ask where he's from.'

'I liked him. I like a challenge.' Again, I wasn't sure I did like the challenge, but I *had* really liked him. I looked his name up on my phone. Andor was Hungarian, meaning manly or brave.

Grace ordered some Apple Sourz shots to unwind. Just as she came back from the bar, Robert with the perfect teeth and straining chest muscles appeared at our table.

'May I join you?'

'Only if you buy us more shots,' said Grace.

'Sure. Why not?' he said, getting another round in.

'So,' Grace challenged him. 'Who do you like best? Me or Caitlin?'

I couldn't believe she was pitting herself against me! 'No, no,' I said to him. 'You don't have to choose now. Dump or Date will let us know in a couple of days.'

'It's fine. I've already chosen,' he said, getting up and walking round to Grace.

As they'd matched, I thought I'd check upstairs for Andor. I still remembered the shiver I'd felt, the electric in his eyes, the tilted smile – but he had already gone. I was surprised he hadn't hung around to see me, almost let down.

By the time I returned, Grace and Robert were kissing. Unfortunately, my coat was on the back of Robert's chair and I had to pull it out from behind him, all the while his lips were locked on Grace's. Even worse, my scarf had slid under the table, probably in embarrassment, and I had to duck down and rummage around. I felt like an interloper to their intimacy, like I was almost trying to get in on the act. As I stood back up I caught sight of the bartender grinning at me, having witnessed my scuffling round at the kissing couple's feet. Total mortification. I fired him a wry smile back, hauling my coat on as I left the table.

'So, did you have a good night?' he asked and there was a hint of sympathy in his voice.

I stopped at the bar. 'Not the greatest.'

'No wonder. You shouldn't have to waste your time speed dating.'

He had a great face I noticed; angular yet there was kindness and humour in the eyes.

'Easy for you to say.'

'The truth is it's always possible to meet people naturally,' he grinned, 'as long as you keep your eyes open.'

There was a sudden flash of connection between us, a bird soaring in the cage of my heart.

He took out a glass and poured me a Corona. I sat down on the barstool and, already, I knew I'd be here for some time.

A STORM ON THE BORDER

The Irish Sea is swelling behind the harbour wall, churning up white foaming flecks in warning semaphores that a storm is on its way. For now, though, the sky is blue, frilled with a few light doilies of cloud. The wind whips against Corey Gillespie's jacket as he watches the first lorry turn into its parking bay. He can tell from the logo that this is the load he's been waiting for all week.

'That was a bitch of a crossing, mate,' the driver says, passing him his papers.

Northern English. Huddersfield, Middlesborough, Hartlepool, thinks Corey, running through his inventory of accents. He shoves the papers into his pocket and climbs up into the back of the lorry. It's easy enough to pluck off the top box which feels light as a feather after the meat trays; it's odd that something so important can feel so light. From up here he can see white-winged waves stretching across the sea as it crashes over shallow red reefs of kelp.

'Won't be long, mate,' he calls to the driver who is sucking on a freshly-lit cigarette in the lee of his cab.

At customs clearance there's a queue. The EU inspector, Anneke, who is doing the checks is infamous for being pernickety, but he needs to get into the guts of this box before clocking-off time so he swings into a shorter queue headed by one of local inspectors. It would deave you the way the crates are slapped down on the metal tables. In front of him a lad is wearing a jacket smeared with leaked animal blood. The smell of raw pork mingled with metallic shellfish nauseates him.

Finally it's his turn. The inspector razor blades through the packing tape, pulls out a few random boxes, gives the contents an ineffectual rummage with his hand and signs the papers. As Corey goes back out to the lorries he notices the sunlight is on the wane and peach contrails are crisscrossing the sky.

The driver spots him in his side mirror and jumps out. Corey clambers into the back and makes a big show of replacing the box while stealthily extracting four small boxes of pills and slipping them into his pocket. The driver looks in the opposite direction as there's a silent understanding of the things that go on in a docking park, a working-class complicity in getting one over on the bosses. Three months in this job and Corey's already an expert conjuror trained in disappearing acts. Not that he's the worst of them. Bobby brings in a bag stuffed with cardboard to make it look full, then refills it with sides of beef and ham. Bobby sells more cuts of meat than the local butchers.

'That's you, mate!' The wind refracts his words as they leave his lips.

The driver shuts the doors, returns to his cab and fires up the engine, while Corey heads to the mobile hut to clock off. The next shift is sitting round the table, geeing themselves up with coffees.

'Watch yourself on the way out,' Bobby tells him. 'There's a dose of them headbangers back on the scene.'

'No worries, Bobby.'

He's feeling the twelve-hour shift in his legs. It's the work boots that wreck him, weighing him down like two black anchors, and no manner of socks will soften the insides of them. He was born with these mad toes that tip up to the sky, fretting their way through every boot he's ever had.

In the car park he changes into his trainers, feeling instantly lighter. He heels himself into his car and sets off, the shades and slants of the sunset exciting him. He loves leaving work when the pale cheek of the sky is rouging and the clouds take on the dusky blue tint of eyeshadow as if ready to go out for the night. This evening, though, dark grey balloons of cloud are beginning to bubble up in the west.

Down the road he spots bright jackets gathered round a small flickering fire bowl, and the sight sends a scurry of alarm into the base of his stomach. He'd hoped the picketing had ended for good, but Bobby was right and the mob are back at the dock entrance, holding a huge 'Larne Says No to Irish Sea Border' banner.

As the barrier lifts, someone waves a Union Jack like a toreador's cape over his windscreen. He hears a fist slam down on his roof and the fear blisters through him.

'Fucking scab!' a man with a bristled chin like a granite crag shouts in at him.

He revs up before they can swamp him and screams past a cop van parked twenty metres away, but it's typical of those useless peelers turning a blind eye to mob rule. Still speeding he joins the main road and turns right at the Jubilee Crown. The next turn takes him up past the Olderfleet Bar. He toots the horn at one of lads standing outside with beers double-parked in his hands and tries to overcome the temptation to quell his nerves with a pint. He's dying to cut loose but as he lowers his speed the image of a Canon camera snaps back into his mind. He's been saving up for months.

Every day he dreams of the shots he could take: the dying sunflowers with their yellow fringes tumbling over the black seeds; the horizon haze where the sun falls on the cold sea; the trees yellow-edged in an earthly reflection of the sun-framed clouds in the evening; and, of course, photos of the anti-Protocolers standing round the flying embers of their fire.

Sometimes he posts his own photos on Instagram but it annoys him how his work colleagues always comment much more on the heavily produced photos by professionals. 'Top photo, mate!' they rave and he wonders if they're pulling his leg by making out that he could have been responsible for a photo with fake starbursts and skies streaked with northern lights.

The fried vinegared smell from a chippy filters into the car and it dawns on him he's starving. He'd eat a horse between two mattresses if he could; he'd eat the beard off Jesus, as his ma would say. The second he thinks of his mother he remembers what he has for her in his pocket. He'd better go there now before the evening runs away with itself. The sooner she gets a dose of pills into her the better. Because of Brexit she's been without them for days.

He drives up Dunboyne Avenue into the older part of town, feeling the car buffeted and pummeled by the wind, trying not to think of the fist on his roof. The kids are throwing firecrackers in a nearby street, the wee hallions. Spits of bright yellow fly out behind the brickwork like welding sparks.

At his ma's the gate is rattling in its sockets, the hasp rasping as he opens it. The Japanese maple in the garden is being winnowed of its red leaves in the dark and the first big drops of rain explode, making him run to the front door.

He's annoyed to find it unlocked. Surely Janice knows to snib it once the last carer has been and gone.

'Hello-o!' he hollers as he enters the hall.

'C'mon in!' shouts Janice from the living room.

Opening the door he can smell the powdery slack from the fire, mixed with something burnt and acrid. The room is worse of a tip than ever.

'Hello, wee darlin'!' greets his ma from her armchair.

He bends down to kiss her, ruffling his cold cheek against hers.

'Go on, Janice,' she urges, 'jazz up that fire for him, would you?'

'Sure it'd roast ye, Ma,' says Janice, not moving an inch from the sofa.

'Ach, you won't even walk the length of yourself these days. You'd do nothing for no one.'

Corey's thinking how Janice is fatter than ever now she's cadging her breakfast and lunch from the nurse who makes her mother's. No wonder she never feels the cold with all that insulation on her bones.

'Guess what I've got for you,' he tells his ma.

'No, I don't believe you!'

'Aye, your ship's come in alright,' he grins, showing her the pills.

'Thank god!'

'I'll get you some water.'

She's barely been able to move since her pills ran out. The MS is swelling her legs up, her ankles are bigger than her knees. The hospital's brought her a bed on wheels, so she doesn't have to climb the stairs every night, but it hurts him to see how she's fading and failing, her bright blue eyes like shrunken blackberries the devil's spat at, as the folktale goes. There are liver spots on her hands that remind him of leaves on the turn. At this rate she'll be gone by the spring, like snow off a ditch.

'That bloody Brexit!' his ma calls through to him. 'I just saw on the news there another fella dying of a heart attack because he'd run out of meds.'

When he comes back in with the water he realises how cold the room is. He bats away the plastic Halloween skeleton hanging from the centre light and gives the fire a good hoke.

'I can't see the tongs, Janice,' he says, stifling a desire to rip the knitting out of her pudgy paws.

The floor's filled with the overflow from a table stacked with Hula Hoops, postcards from Hillsborough, photos of Prince Harry and other sundry objects beginning with an 'H' to fit in with Janice's H for Halloween theme. HRH Prince Harry is the most prominent H of all. It takes Corey a few seconds to work out that a packet of Ginger Snaps must allude to Harry's red hair. Even the t-shirt she's wearing is emblazoned with Harry's huge image and his unlikely words 'I love you, honeybunch. Can't wait to have tea with you x.' But there's no talking to Janice about such matters. She makes the most OCD person in the world look normal.

He shakes out what's in the scuttle into the orange heart of the fire.

'I haven't a notion what's happened to them tongs,' says Janice looking round the room through her large doll-blue eyes.

'It'll be that Prince Harry swiping them. Him and his wife are always after the freebies.'

'Ach, don't start her off,' beseeches his mother.

'Harry's welcome to them,' says Janice. 'He says he's coming to Larne next week and taking me out. Mebbie for tea or a fry, I don't know yet.'

'Well, I'm sure he'll be very impressed by your shrine. It's not Halloween, but Harryeen!'

'Oh, sure, laugh away, you, but Harry and me have big plans.'

'Ach, would you give over,' says his ma. 'He's married to Meghan.'

'Aye, you've some rival there, Janice.'

'What's "rival"? I've never heard of that before.'

'A rival is like a competitor.'

'Rival.' Her eyes are suddenly focused and luminous. 'I'm going to write that down ... I love words.'

Sometimes it makes him wonder if she could have been a writer had she not been starved of oxygen at birth. It's impossible to follow the labyrinthine paths of her mind. He never knows how much she truly believes in her fleeting love affairs with celebrities, or if she's taking the hand out of everyone. There is surprising intelligence behind her limitations, a strange elision like a sun moving in and out of an eclipse. At other times her pupils roll into the corners of her eyes, leaving an expanse of white that reminds him of a marble statue.

'I saw on the news the protestors are back,' says his ma.

'I know. They thumped my car as I went past.'

'Christ,' she shivers. 'You better make sure your doors are locked.'

'Sure, he's tough as nails, Ma,' says Janice, reaching over and giving him a playful punch in the stomach. 'See? Tight as a drum.'

'Aye, you'd think I was wearing a stab vest,' he laughs, thumping his own chest muscles. 'Anyway, I'm heading on here. Janice, come on and lock the door behind me.'

He kisses his ma and heads out into the hall where he confronts Janice.

'Did you put plastic in the fire again?'

'Aye, but only a wee totie pick of it.'

He's told her a million times not to burn plastic bags. In that wind they could blow up the chimney. He's not forgotten the time two years ago Janice set the chimney ablaze and the fire engine only just managed to save the house. If a fire breaks out now his mother can't even help put it out, never mind escape.

But Janice won't be told. And it isn't her fault, his mother always tells him, begging him to be patient.

On the night she gave birth to Janice thirty years ago, there was a blue riot going on outside and the ambulance couldn't get through. Already in labour, she had to be lifted into the back of a police land rover. But the land rover was too slow for her, mobbed and petrol-bombed as it was by the crowd, and the baby wouldn't wait. Janice came out half-strangled by the cord with no medics to intervene, just young police officers who swore and cursed in horror. By the time they reached the hospital it was too late to reverse the damage.

'See you, rival!' Janice calls out cheekily as he runs to the car.

From the window of the hut Corey can see the geese walking along the shoreline and feeding on the kelp. There are mounds of decaying seaweed on the beach, studded with the corpses of white crabs, belly up and glimmering with metal bags shorn from the oyster beds. He watches the ferry turn towards the dock. It's running late after the storm.

On the other side of the shore a convoy of white police vans are on their way to relieve the previous shift. The protestors were more subdued this morning when he drove past. Only about fifteen had made it out of their beds. Fair-weather revolutionaries they were alright. And who cares what they think anyway? He doesn't give a fuck if the sea border leads to an united Ireland. As far as jobs go this is the most pay he's ever had and he's happy as a sandfly, sitting bantering with the other stevedores till the tide brings in the next consignment of lorries.

The sea is still now, the gulls leaving feathering trails in the water as their feet skim the surface. There are bangs and whirrs as the ferry ramp is cranked open, prompting a stir in the hut.

'Lay down your teabags, lads,' winks Bobby, throwing his last dregs of tea down the sink. 'Here comes the sausage invasion!'

They hurry outside as the first of the lorries trundles into the unloading bay.

'Lamb chops. That one's mine!' says Bobby, salivating. His outsize coat has more pockets than a poacher's.

'Corey!'

One of the managers of Shed 66, Dale, is beckoning him over. There is something about Dale's raised eyebrows and the grim set of his lips that sends Corey's chest spiralling.

'Just a word in your ear,' Dale tells him. 'We had a call from Kearney Medical and they're short on stock. You were the one responsible for the documentation, so do you know anything about it?'

Oh god, he had got too greedy! As well as yesterday's pills he'd swiped some painkillers, bringing two packets to his mother and doling out another dozen to Bobby and the lads. But it was hardly a case of him ripping the arse out of it. He could make hundreds on the black market if he went wild.

'No, I don't know anything. Mebbie it was the driver or one of the loaders who pinched them.'

'Fine,' says Dale, nodding, but there's a degree of doubt in his voice. 'We just have to make sure none of our staff are accused. From now on we'll be doing bag searches at the end of every shift.'

Corey is shaking as he walks away. A beechnut cracks under his boot. A seagull is squealing out as it wheels overhead. 'Thiieeeff, thiieeeff, thiiiiieeeff!' goes its cry.

But there's no time to worry about it as he's caught up in the checks, climbing up into lorry after lorry. Soon the sea is starting to reflect the darkening of the afternoon sky. There's barely a whisk of a white cap on its benign surface.

He's carrying a heavy tray of salmon up to the warehouse when Bobby runs over.

'Hey, Corey. Look over there!'

He turns, tilting his chin up, and spots a lone angry cloud turning mauve in the sunset. Suddenly he realises it's smoke.

'It's from your ma's street,' says Bobby. 'My mate just told me.'

'Oh, shit!'

Corey quickly calls his ma. The tone rings on; it's not like her to ignore it. He remembers the smell of last night's burning plastic and it fills him with fear.

'Clock out for me,' he tells Bobby, setting down the tray.

'Careful of the protest!' Bobby shouts after him.

He runs down towards the carpark. He should clear it with Dale first, but he's swept up in his own sense of emergency. He starts up the car, his boots clumsily revving as he reverses out. He has to be there for his mother. Sure, she can barely walk. Oh, please don't let it be Janice and Ma, he prays.

He speeds along by the harbour until he can see the gauntlet waiting for him, standing by a fire drum. The lamp post behind them is a totem pole of angry posters. Fuck them, just relics from the Troubles. They seem feverish, someone keeps stabbing a placard into the air, and that granite-chinned guy who thinks he's the hardman moves to the front of his troops.

Corey is pulling up at the barrier as his phone rings. He drags it out of his pocket.

'Hello?' goes Janice's voice uncertainly

The barrier is slowly raised. His phone's in his left hand and he knows he should hurry and lift the handbrake, but he has to know if his mother's safe.

'Janice, is there a fire?'

He can see on his periphery the man swoop in on his door. At the click of the handle he realises he never locked it and, as the door swings open, the phone falls to the floor and he can hear Janice say 'kids ... fireworks on the roof ... but we're both fine,' and he isn't fine as his head is punched again and again by the granite man with rocks of knuckles. And he looks out to the police land rovers and through their tiny shaded windows the officers watch and do nothing, just as years ago they barely helped his mother, and he can't breathe anymore, there's nothing in his lungs, his head is so light and soaring like a seagull leaving the anger far below. And the second before his eyes snap shut the sky is full of starbursts.

'Corey, are you there?' Janice's voice trails from the phone. 'Prince Harry just called, the wee honey. Says he's on his way right now to put out the fire.'

Rosemary Jenkinson is a playwright, poet and fiction writer from Belfast. She taught English in Greece, France, the Czech Republic and Poland before returning to Belfast in 2002. Her plays include *The Bonefire* (Stewart Parker BBC Radio Award), *Planet Belfast, Here Comes the Night, Michelle and Arlene, May the Road Rise Up* and *Lives in Translation*. Her plays have been performed in Dublin, London, Edinburgh, Brussels, New York, Washington DC and Belfast. Arlen House publish her latest plays *Billy Boy* (2022) and *Silent Trade* (2023).

In 2018 she received a Major Artist Award from the Arts Council of Northern Ireland. She was writer-in-residence at the Lyric Theatre Belfast in 2017 and at the Leuven Centre for Irish Studies in 2019. Her short story collections include *Contemporary Problems Nos. 53 & 54, Aphrodite's Kiss, Catholic Boy* (shortlisted for the EU Prize for Literature), *Lifestyle Choice 10mgs* (shortlisted for the Edge Hill Short Story Prize) and the bestselling *Marching Season* published by Arlen House in 2021.

The *Irish Times* praised her for 'an elegant wit, terrific characterisation and an absolute sense of her own particular Belfast'.